FINDING FELICITY

The Gold Coast Retrievers, Book 5

P. CREEDEN

© 2018, P. Creeden.

All rights reserved. Except as permitted under the U.S. Copyright Act of 1976, no part of this publication may be reproduced, distributed or transmitted in any form or by any means, or stored in a database or retrieval system without the prior written permission of the publisher.

This is a work of fiction. Names, characters, organizations, places, events, and incidents are either products of the author's imagination or are used fictitiously. Any resemblance to actual persons, living or dead, or actual events is purely coincidental.

No part of this work may be reproduced, or stored in a retrieval system, or transmitted in any form or by any means, electronic, mechanical, photocopying, recording, or otherwise, without written permission of the publisher.

Sweet Promise Press
PO Box 72
Brighton, MI 48116

※ Created with Vellum

Chapter One

"SHAKE, JJ," little Addison commanded, holding a hand out to the golden retriever.

The three-year-old golden retriever set his paw in the palm of her hand, eliciting an excited giggle from Addison. Felicity couldn't help but smile at the little eight-year-old girl. Addison had been diagnosed as mildly autistic and had a hard time making eye contact with people or talking with anyone outside of her family. But she'd begun to open up to Felicity's dog, Jay, or JJ as Addison called him, over the past week. She'd even interacted with Felicity on occasion, although she had kept her eyes on the golden. It was still a win.

This was the reason she loved her job. Though Addison hadn't gone up much in her reading comprehension, she was interacting with Jay, which was all that really mattered. She smiled down on Addison, wanting to pat the girl on the shoulder, but Addison would shy away at Felicity's touch. Instead, Felicity patted the dog's head while she spoke to the girl. "You did great today, Addison. I'm so proud of you. JJ is super proud of you, too. He can't wait to hear what happens to the brown bear next. Will you try to read ahead and practice so that next time you can tell JJ more of the story?"

The little girl nodded, her eyes never leaving the golden retriever's. Then she took hold of the small book and pulled it to her chest, running off in the direction of her other classmates as they headed outside for recess.

Felicity knew that Addison would practice hard so that she could share more of the story with Jay. The simple fact of knowing that JJ was waiting to hear more from her would be a big enough motivation. Jay always listened and sat still. He never criticized her or the other children when they stumbled upon a word. His patience knew no bounds, and the kids trusted him.

After giving Jay a scratch behind the ears, Felicity stood up from her cross-legged position on the floor mat. Her muscles were a bit stiff from sitting too long, but she wasn't about to change position when one of her students tried hard to increase their comprehension. If they got a hint that she was being impatient with them, they'd quit trying. It was the nature of working with special needs children.

"How did today go?" Mr. Jordan, the vice principal, asked with a wan half-smile and a raised eyebrow.

Felicity's chest tightened. He'd snuck up on her as he was apt to do, asking the same question each time. She knew how this conversation would go, nearly by heart. She turned toward him with the biggest smile she could muster. "Very well. I think I made excellent progress with all of my students today."

He scratched his chin. "And how many students did you work with today?"

She swallowed before answering. "Four."

He nodded his head, his mouth twisting as he narrowed his eyes at her. "Four students." He gestured toward Jay. "All of this… to help just four students. Seems like an inefficient way of doing things."

And with those words, her heart sank to her stomach. She cleared her throat, her arms crossing over her chest. "These children need alternative methods to the mainstream way of doing things, to combat their difficulties with learning. These methods may not seem efficient for the time being, but they will pay off in the long run."

He sighed. "I guess time will tell. Meanwhile, keep that dog on a leash, even in the classroom. We can't have him biting a child."

"He would never—"

"Any dog will bite, depending on the situation. And Gold Coast Elementary doesn't need the premiums on our insurance increasing. Just do as I ask and keep him on a leash. Understood?"

Felicity felt the anger boiling within her, heating her cheeks. Jay had sat beside her the entire time with his tail wagging while watching the exchange. She didn't usually keep a leash on him when he sat in the reading nook with children, because the bookshelves provided a physical barrier. The children connected with the dog better without interference from the leash. She pulled the leather lead from her pocket and snapped it on Jay's collar without another word.

The wan smile returned—in fact, Mr. Jordan's whole pallor was colorless and his mannerisms stiff. Nothing about him seemed healthy or happy. He turned away and headed toward the classroom door, and Felicity chided herself for thinking badly of the man. Maybe he wasn't happy because of health issues. Maybe he had a hard home life. Her mother would have scolded her and told her that if she saw a problem, she should work to fix it instead of criticizing. The man might need extra vitamin C or something to help his health. She made a mental note to order him a basket of oranges or some other kind of fruit. The thought made her smile. Her mother was right. Helping in a situation like this was the better way to go. It made her feel more human to think about helping.

But maybe she should send it anonymously, so he wouldn't think any strings were attached. Yeah. And she wouldn't want him to think she was flirting with him or something either. After all, he was a single man, as far as she knew. Even if he was fifteen years her senior, you never knew.

The digital clock on the wall declared it was nearly one o'clock. Felicity scoffed at the large red numbers. When she was a child in school, they still had analog clocks. Would she have ever learned how to read the time on a real clock without the desperation of wondering when the next bell would ring?

As if on cue, the bell rang.

With a small nod of her head to the teacher, Mrs. Morris, Felicity and Jay headed out the door. The hallways were full of small children holding onto a rope and staying in lines on one side of the hallway or the other. Some of the children squealed in excitement at seeing the golden retriever walking down the hallway of their elementary school. Many of the children even called out his name. Jay held his head a little higher, wagged his tail in a steady rhythm with his walk, and smiled at the children with his tongue lolling. A few hands reached out and touched his fur as the pair passed, and Felicity just smiled at the children.

Her smile fell the moment she got to the front door of the school building. Storm clouds gathered in the west, and the slightest drops of rain began to fall. The poor children would have to come in from their recess. Felicity loosened her grip on her leash and dashed toward her SUV. By the time she loaded Jay in the truck and got herself behind the wheel, the rain began in earnest.

Before cranking her car, she peered through the windshield. Just past the dark line of clouds, the sun was already shining. This short storm wouldn't last more than twenty minutes. Hardly enough to help the drought they'd been dealing with since the end of summer. Felicity pushed wisps of blonde hair out of her face. Her signature ponytail had gotten a little loose when she'd made her run for her car. She pulled it free and found that her holder's elastic had been stretched a little thin. Next time she made it to the store, she needed to pick up another pack.

In the meantime, she pushed her hair up into a messy bun and used the holder to keep the hair back. Then she started her vehicle. Before she pulled out of the parking lot, the rain had stopped.

Early autumn in Redwood Cove had always been one of Felicity's favorite times of year. The weather was still warm enough to roll down the windows in her truck, but Felicity was always careful to put JJ's window down halfway, so he couldn't lean too far out of it.

The short storm had brought with it a cool breeze and temperature drop. The drive home, past the marina, to the quiet neighborhood, not too far from the dog park, was pleasant. Here she and her roommate rented a small ranch house with fenced backyard for Jay.

She frowned at the silver sedan parked across the street, in front of her neighbor's yard, as she pulled into her driveway. The car seemed out of place. Almost no one parked on the street this time of day, and her neighbors didn't have a sedan like that one.

Once she stepped out of the vehicle and let JJ down, she glanced in the direction of the silver sedan again and watched as a tall, dark, and handsome man crossed the street with his gaze focused on her.

As any young woman living alone would do, Felicity went through the reasons why this man might be approaching her so suddenly. Then she noticed his police badge attached to the belt loop of his pants. Her heart skipped a beat. Even though she'd never broken a law in her entire life, Felicity found her stomach tightening into a knot as she realized the man was a police officer.

There was no reason to panic. Maybe he just wanted to ask her a question about the neighbors across the street. "Sit," she commanded JJ in a shaky voice and tried to swallow past the lump in her throat. But her mouth was too dry.

The police officer's face softened as he stepped into her driveway, and he called out to her, "Excuse me. Are you Felicity Stilton?"

Ice filled her stomach. This was about her... not the Wilsons from across the street. Her heart beat harder and her ears rang as her blood pressure rose. JJ looked up at her and whined. She blinked and nodded slightly, suddenly unable to speak.

Worry lines formed on the police officer's brow. "Miss, are you okay?"

Spots crowded her vision, and she closed her eyes, leaning against the SUV. Stars popped behind her lids.

A warm hand rested on her shoulder. "Miss Stilton?"

Jay yipped.

A fire lit somewhere deep in the darkness of Felicity's mind. Really? A police officer approached her, and she felt faint? What century did she live in again? Anger fueled the flame at the pit of her stomach. Blood rushed to her cheeks and warmed them as she snapped open her eyes and straightened. Her hands fisted as she steeled herself. "Is there something I can help you with, officer?"

He blinked at her a moment and then nodded. "I'm Detective Willis with the Redwood Cove Police Department. I'm afraid I have some bad news. Is there somewhere quiet we can discuss this? I think you should have a seat."

The fear turned her stomach cold again, dousing the fire that she'd had a moment before.

She wasn't a manic person, normally, but right now, she had little control over her emotions. She swallowed. "I'm fine, Detective. Please continue."

His maple brown eyes assessed her from head to toe. She would have been offended if she'd been looked at this way by almost any other man, but she got the feeling that instead of checking her out, the officer was trying to determine whether she was truthful, or maybe if she could handle what he was about to say. When his eyes met hers again, he nodded. "I regret to inform you that we found a body this morning that appears to belong to your mother."

The earth shifted beneath Felicity's feet, but she steadied herself with a hand on the roof of her truck. Panic clawed its way up her spine. "What?"

The officer grabbed her by the elbow. "Are you sure you're okay? Maybe we should at least sit on the porch."

She straightened and shook off his hold on her elbow. Her mother? What kind of accident could she have gotten into? Where was her father? "Is my father okay?"

His brow furrowed. "Your mother was married?"

She blinked at him, feeling her own brow

scrunch. "Of course she was married. Didn't you go to her house first? My father would have been there. I don't understand why you're coming here to tell me instead of him ... if he wasn't involved in an accident with her?"

The detective drew up taller, staring at her for a moment. Then he let out a slow breath. "I believe we have a misunderstanding. Your mother's name was Elizabeth Collier?"

Relief warred with sadness as her heart squeezed in her chest. He hadn't been talking about her real mother—the one who adopted her and raised her and loved her. He'd been talking about her birth mother. Slowly, she nodded, talking past the lump that had lodged in her throat. "Yes, Liz is my mother."

He nodded slowly with her. "And according to our records, she wasn't married, and you're her only living relative."

The back of her jaw hurt as she ground her molars. "Yes, that's right."

"Then could I ask you to come with me to identify the body?"

The blood drained and left her lightheaded. He wanted her to identify Liz's body. Liz, who Felicity had only known for the past six years, since she'd turned eighteen and had sought her out. They'd eaten lunch together a handful of times, but Liz had been too busy with her vineyard, and Felicity had been chasing her own dreams. They'd never really had the time to get to know each other well, and now that opportunity was gone.

The detective cleared his throat. "I believe it would be best if I drove you. This is sudden news, and it's not safe to drive in a compromised emotional state."

She blinked at him, her hand fisting on Jay's leash. "I... It's too short a notice. I don't have anyone to watch my dog."

He blinked at the golden retriever, and then knelt to get on the level with Jay. He scratched the dog behind the ears. "Are you a good boy? Want to go for a car ride?"

Jay stood and wagged his tail in response. It pleased Felicity that he took an immediate liking to the man. It helped relieve some of the anxiety that had tightened her chest.

Detective Willis stood once more. "He can go for a ride with us, although he may need to stay in the car while we're at the coroner's. I'll find a shady spot."

Felicity nodded slowly again and then followed the detective toward his unmarked sedan.

DARREN COULDN'T SHAKE the feeling that there was something familiar about Felicity Stilton. Even her name almost rang a bell in the back of his mind, but he pushed it off. Maybe he'd seen her around town. Or he could have even pulled her over back when he made traffic stops. But now he was a rookie detective, so the last thing he wanted to do was ask the young woman where he might know her from.

Instead, he drove her to the coroner's office in relative silence. He'd allowed the music of the radio to provide easy listening in the background of the drive, but he could barely hear it well enough to recognize the lyrics. When they pulled up into the shadiest space in the parking lot, Darren looked over at his charge.

Felicity had her dark blonde hair pulled back in a messy bun. A few wisps escaped and cascaded down the back of her neck. The girl had a bit of a tan that made him feel she must have liked to spend a lot of time outdoors. Her sporty outfit gave her an athletic feel. Her blue eyes met his, full of emotions—confusion, fear, grief.

He let down each of the windows several inches. Luckily, the rain they'd had earlier had brought with it a bit of a cold front, leaving Redwood Cove a balmy, seventy-something degrees for the afternoon. Glancing in the rearview mirror, he checked the back seat where the golden retriever seemed to smile back at him.

"How did my mother die?" Felicity asked, finally.

Darren felt better that, this time, they were at least sitting in the car. He took a deep breath. "Your mother was on several different medications. It appeared that she overdosed on her sleeping pills, but we won't know for sure until we get the coroner's toxicology report back."

Wrinkles appeared over her brows. "So, it was an accident?"

He shook his head slowly. "She was found at her kitchen table. By all accounts, it appears to be suicide."

She blinked hard, and tears welled in the bottom of her eyelids. "I can't believe it."

An accident was always one thing, but suicide was quite another. Darren had already experienced how families reacted to both. No one wanted to accept either outcome, but to believe that a loved one could take their own life seemed too great a burden to bear. After she swiped at her eyes, she looked out the front windshield. It made sense that she'd need a moment to process this new information, and Darren was going to give it to her.

A cool breeze blew in through the window and across the skin of his forearm. He'd known what it was like to deal with death in the family--his own mother had died when he was a teenager. But there was something that bothered him about the way that this woman had first reacted to the news of her mother's death. "Did you have a close relationship with your mother?"

Still looking out the front of the vehicle, Felicity shook her head. "Not with Liz, no. Liz is my birth mother, but she gave me up for adoption pretty much as soon as I was born. I'm very close with my real mother—my adoptive parents are great."

"Oh," he managed. That made sense now. The confusion of their first conversation became clear. "Do your parents live in Redwood Cove? Should we give them a call and let them know what's going on? The support of family could be good when times are hard."

Her blue eyes met his. "I'll call my dad once I identify the body for you. He'll help me make arrangements for the funeral and fill out whatever paperwork I need."

"As far as I know, you're the sole heir of your mother's... I mean Elizabeth Collier's estate. She'll need you to settle that and see to her vineyard as well."

She blinked several times. "She owned the vineyard? I thought she just worked there."

Darren shrugged. "I don't know all the specifics, but I'm pretty sure she owned it, as her name is on the sign leading to the vineyard. But you'll have to see her lawyer to find out for certain."

Her eyes closed again, and she took several deep breaths and leaned back against the car seat. This was a lot to handle at once. Darren understood that. When she opened her eyes, she leaned forward and pulled on the door handle. "I'm ready."

Chapter Two
_____

"YES, THAT'S LIZ." Felicity wrapped her arms around herself and turned around, away from the familiar face. The air conditioning was still up in the morgue, as if they needed to keep the place extra cool, like a refrigerator, for the bodies.

The morbid thought gave her chills. She'd tried to look at Liz's face as little as she could. Felicity didn't want to remember her birth mother as the dead body that laid on the cold metal table in the morgue. Instead, she'd rather remember the woman who had an easy-going laugh, crooked bottom teeth that only showed when she smiled wide, and perfect hair, which never seemed to be out of place. The woman had been all business each time that they met but seemed to open up to Felicity after they'd spent a little time together.

Nothing about her mother had seemed overly emotional or depressed, but did she really know Liz well enough to judge? Felicity didn't live with the woman and couldn't really presume to know her like that. Still, it was a hard pill to swallow—ugh. No pun intended. Inwardly, Felicity kicked herself at the play on words.

Detective Willis led her outside and next door to the police station and toward a row of desks in an open area. He guided her to the seat across from him and began pushing a few forms her direction. "I'm sorry, but I need for you to sign these so that we can release the body to the funeral home. And the few personal effects she had on her are in this small box."

Felicity took the box and found only Liz's watch, a pair of earrings, and a set of house keys. She sighed, eyeing the digital fitness tracker that Liz used as a watch. On Felicity's arm was a similar tracker. They'd been friends on the social media app attached to the tracker—and on Reel Life where they shared pictures with each other. Social media was how they stayed in touch for the most part. The tracker's app showed her mother had consistently gotten over her ten-thousand steps each day. Liz usually tried for double, but that was her competitive nature. Her mother wouldn't have steps recorded on those charts any longer. A little bit of emptiness would replace where she'd felt her mother interacted with her on a daily basis although they were on different sides of the county.

She blinked up at the detective and found his maple brown eyes on hers. His smile was soft, and the slightest dimple appeared on the side of his mouth. She forced a smile. "Thank you so much for all your help. I'll give my father a call and see if he can pick me up from here. I don't want to put you through too much trouble, Detective Willis."

"No trouble. And you can call me Darren."

No way. Her heart skipped a beat. "Darren Willis?"

He quirked an eyebrow at her. "That's my name."

"Do you have a brother named Kent?" Now that she was looking at him, she could see the resemblance—the same dark skin, the same light in his eyes, the same square jaw and broad shoulders.

His brow furrowed. "Yes, I have two younger brothers."

"Kent and Tony."

He laughed. "Redwood Cove is a small town."

"I went to high school with Kent. We were both freshman when you were a senior." And she used to have the biggest crush on Darren, but she wouldn't admit to that part. Not in a million years. She would have thought that time would have helped her get over her schoolgirl crush, but her heart had other plans as it sped up from just the fact he was so close to her.

He nodded. "You did look a bit familiar. You and Kent were friends?"

"I was best friends with his girlfriend, Monique."

He laughed. "I remember you. Glasses and braces, right?"

Her nose scrunched, and she really wished he didn't remember that part.

"But wait. I thought Monique's friend's name was Felicia."

Blood rushed to her face, and prickles ran across the skin of her arms. He had made that mistake when they'd first met, calling her Felicia. And she'd never corrected him. For nearly a year before he went to off to college, he called her the wrong name, and the one time that Monique noticed, she'd picked on Felicity so hard for her letting him slide without correction. She shook her head slightly. "It's always been Felicity."

He laughed, his eyes sparkling as he looked at her appreciatively. "Well, you're all grown up now."

The blush in her skin deepened. She needed to change the subject before her heart exploded. "So how is Kent?"

Everything in the room seemed out of focus except for Darren's smiling face. Her heart ached when she eyed that dimple again. A few moments before, when she didn't know who he was, she'd appreciated that he was a very handsome man, but now that she knew, she couldn't get her emotions under control.

"Married to Monique. They are expecting their second child here in about a month."

She blinked and shook her head. "Wow."

"I guess you didn't keep in touch with Monique?"

She scratched her head a bit. "Well, we went different ways after high school. I haven't really talked to anyone from back in those days."

He nodded. "Makes sense. It's not like I have much to do with the crowd I ran with back then either."

"Yeah. That's true." Not that she really knew,

but it felt like the right thing to say. She really needed to get away. Too much blood had been rushing to her face for too long, and suddenly the air in the room didn't seem so cold anymore. "Do you mind if I leave this box here a moment? And can you point me in the direction of the restroom?"

He stood and gestured in the direction of a sign that named the Ladies' room. "Right over there."

She shuffled toward the door, tripping over nothing and catching herself on the side of his desk. He'd reached out his hands to help steady her, but she pulled back from his touch. "I'm fine. Thanks."

Nothing could stop her from getting to that room of respite and escape from the fool she was making of herself. Once she'd slipped into the bathroom and shut the door, she let out a long breath she didn't know she'd been holding. She panted for a moment. What was wrong with her? How could her heart be pining over her first love… her first crush, just because she'd run into him at the worst possible moment? Liz was dead. Felicity had an estate to settle. And right now, she didn't have time for schoolgirl crushes. She needed to get home and away from Darren before she lost all sense of herself.

With a deep breath, she pulled out her cell phone and dialed her father's cell phone number.

DARREN SHOOK his head and laughed. Little Felicia grew up—make that Felicity. Why on Earth did she never correct him if he was saying her name wrong? He remembered the shy girl who came over a few times to hang out with Monique and Kent. She'd hardly make eye contact with him back then. She giggled a lot. Looking at the woman in front of him now, he could see a vague resemblance, especially in her blush, but she'd certainly blossomed into a beautiful woman. That much was for sure.

When she walked out of the bathroom, her blue eyes were focused at the white tile flooring of the police station while her brows knitted together. He stood and met her halfway. "Are you okay?" he asked.

Her brow softened as her gaze rose to meet his. Confident, strong. Not the shy mouse she'd been in high school. She smiled self-deprecatingly. "My parents are out of town on a business trip—in Korea. They told me about their plans a month ago, and I forgot. It'll be two more weeks before they get back in town. My mom offered to leave on the first flight back and come help me, but I told her to stay. They almost never get to travel, and the last thing I want to do is ruin their trip."

Darren nodded. "I understand that… How about you let me help you? I can drive you over to the vineyard now. I have the number of your mother's lawyer. I can call him and have him meet us over at the vineyard."

More than one emotion flickered across Felicity's face. Her cheeks colored, and she looked away shyly for a moment. "I can't take you away from your work like that. I'm sure you must be busy."

The shy girl had returned. He kind of liked the dichotomy of what she'd become and what she used to be. And the way they intermingled now made him respect her and want to protect her at the same time. "It's no trouble. Your mother's case hasn't quite been closed yet, so until it is, it's my priority."

She looked up at him and smiled. "If you're sure."

"I'm sure." He smiled back at her and sat back down at his desk, fishing through the paperwork to find the lawyer's business card. His gaze slipped over toward his lieutenant, who was on the phone with his back turned toward them. It would be best if Darren hurried with this phone call and got out the door before the lieutenant asked him where he was going. This was supposed to be an open and shut case of suicide, and the police lieutenant wouldn't like for it to take Darren all day.

But right now, every part of him wanted to help Felicity in her time of need—not just because he knew who she was, but because this was his first case and he wanted to be as thorough as possible. At least that's what he told himself as he glanced over at her pretty blue eyes once more.

Chapter Three

BEAUTIFUL ROWS of grapevines decorated both sides of the long driveway into Dorma Valley Winery. The sun had already lowered toward the horizon, coloring the sky a lighter shade of purple, contrasting with the dark color of the grapes. Felicity sighed. She'd only been to the winery once on invitation when she'd first turned twenty-one.

Her birthday had been near the end of the summer leading into her senior year in college. Because Felicity had never been to a wine tasting, and was finally of age to do it, Liz had invited her over on her birthday. Dorma Valley wine did tastings several times a month, and her birth mother had planned one specifically on her birthday.

Which, in theory, was very sweet. But in practice, it was another matter.

The woman had been so busy running the winery that day, Felicity and Liz had barely greeted each other at the beginning of the tour and tasting and didn't even say goodbye at the end. Felicity had eaten cheese and downed a few glasses of wine, left with the tour group on the bus, and then taken a cab home to her parents' house. The best part about that day was when she got home, her parents had a golden retriever puppy waiting for her—Jay.

Felicity turned in her seat to pat Jay on the head at the memory. It had broken her heart back then that the same woman who'd been too busy to raise her as a baby couldn't even take the time to celebrate a birthday with her as an adult. Before that time, Felicity's adoptive parents had asked her to invite Liz to all their holiday gatherings, but Liz had never made the time to attend. After that day, even though her parents had continued to ask her to invite the woman, Felicity had stopped bothering her. In fact, most of their lunch dates had happened before that birthday… Felicity wasn't sure if they'd had another one after.

Gravel crunched under the tires of the unmarked police sedan as they drove up into the lot of the vineyard. Two other cars sat parked side by side up against the main store area, where Felicity had been the one time for the tour. The large sign on the store declared it "Dorma Valley Wine, established 1992," and a small sign at the bottom said, "Elizabeth Collier, proprietor." The smaller sign seemed somewhat newer and hadn't been there the last time Felicity had been. Jay whined in the backseat.

Although she wasn't sure if dogs were allowed at the winery, there was an open field between the store and the main house that seemed the perfect place to let Jay out to stretch his legs. Felicity felt for the leash in her pocket, and when Darren hopped out of the vehicle, she did the same, opening the back door and letting the three-year-old golden out and pointed him toward the field in front of them.

His burst of joy was like sunlight on clouds of sadness and bitterness that had overwhelmed Felicity on the drive up—at the memories she had of Liz, the insecurities of being abandoned by the woman, and the fact that there would never be any real relationship between them. Jay ran circles around the field as though he'd never been to such an open place with so many new smells.

"Excuse me. You can't have that dog here," a

skinny, older gentleman with glasses said as he came up toward them. He gave her a stern look, and his pale pallor reminded her of Mr. Jordan's.

She was about to apologize and call Jay over when behind him the door to the store opened again, and a shorter, squatter man with a mustache came out. "Curtis, she's fine. This is the woman I was just telling you about. Felicity, right?"

A frown tugged down on her lips, but she did her best to force it back into a smile, at least a little bit of one. "Yes, that's me."

The man with a mustache nodded, hooking his thumbs into his belt loops. "I figured as much. And this must be Detective Willis. I spoke to you on the phone, detective." He reached out a hand for Darren to shake. "I'm Lucian Wright, the lawyer." He gestured toward the tall, pale man who still continued to frown at Felicity. "This is Curtis Page. He's the supervisor of the winery."

Darren shook hands with the lawyer and then offered a hand toward Mr. Page, but Mr. Page didn't even glance Darren's direction. He was still too busy scowling at Jay. With a lift of his eyebrow, Darren withdrew his hand and put it in the pocket of his jeans. "Nice to meet you both."

"Could you please put that animal on a leash?" Mr. Page huffed and crossed his arms over his chest.

Felicity whistled, and Jay stopped in his tracks and lifted his head to look at her but stood stock still. "Come on, Jay!"

He took a moment to think about whether he wanted to come. Felicity swallowed. Although Jay was one of the best-behaved dogs she knew, it was times like this, when he'd felt he hadn't run enough, or played enough at the dog park, when she'd call him, and he needed to take a moment to consider whether he wanted to come or not. It made him seem less well-behaved than he actually was. She patted her leg. "Come on!"

Jay broke through his statuesque moment and came running straight toward her. When he was younger, his brakes weren't as good, and he'd nearly bent back her knee when he'd run into her legs. Now she'd taken the habit of widening her stance to allow the golden to run between her legs and come back around to her as he did now. He panted as he looked up at her as she snapped the leash onto his collar.

Mr. Wright slapped his hands together and offered her a smile. "Well, why don't we step inside and get this paperwork filled out so I can release the estate into your capable hands, young lady?"

The taller man's scowl deepened. "We can't have that animal in the store. It's a health code violation."

"Of course, it is." Mr. Wright rolled his eyes. "Just wait at one of the tables out here on the covered porch. I'll head inside and bring the paperwork out to you."

Darren stayed right with Felicity as she walked across the lot, keeping himself between her and Mr. Page, who hadn't stopped scowling at her and Jay since they'd arrived. Once they reached the table, Darren pulled out a chair for her and then sat in the one immediately next to her at the round table. Jay lay down next to the chair where she sat.

Mr. Wright came right back out with a clipboard and several papers. "Your mother was the sole proprietor of the winery. Her vice-president, Heath Anderson, is on his way back from a business trip in Napa now. Her will states that everything she owned, including the winery, was to go to you upon her death. Your mother had no debts, and the winery itself is in the black. So, this is quite a fortuitous day for you, young lady."

Felicity frowned. "Fortuitous?"

Mr. Wright's mouth twisted between a frown and a smile and then he shrugged but didn't say another word.

After closing her eyes a moment and taking a deep breath, she looked down at the papers in front of her. For a few seconds, the letters in front of her looked like a jumbled mass of unrecognizable words. She felt like a grade-schooler again, where her dyslexia had control of her instead of the other way around. Her emotions had seized her and taken her in a direction she didn't want to go. She didn't want to break down in front of all these men.

This day was far from fortuitous. She didn't want to be here. She didn't want to own the winery or deal with Liz's estate. When she'd woken up this morning, this wasn't what she'd planned to do with her day. How could things have turned out like this? Tears made her vision blurry, but she swiped at her eyes to get them out of her way. She needed to focus so that she could make sense out of the contracts that she had in front of her. There was no way that her father would want her to sign anything without reading it first.

A long sigh expelled from over her head, forcing her to glance up. Curtis Page continued to frown, but this time his scowl was pointed in Mr. Wright's direction. "If you have no further need of me, I've got other things I should be doing."

The lawyer nodded. "Of course. We're fine as we are. Right, Felicity?"

She blinked up at him. "Right. I'll just need a few more minutes to read through all this."

A warm hand settled on her shoulder. She looked up into Darren's brown eyes as he smiled at her. "Take your time. No one is trying to rush you."

Mr. Page cleared his throat, and then started away, his lips clamped together. Before he'd gotten too far, however, he flicked on the overhead lights recessed in the wood of the covered porch. Inwardly Felicity thanked him, as the words on the page became clearer and easier to focus on in the improved lighting.

She read through the pages and found nothing that she disagreed with terribly, so after several minutes, she put the pen to the page and signed where red ink had circled. The moment she'd finished, another car came rushing into the lot— one of those luxury brand sedans that nearly looked like a sports car, kicking up a gravel dust cloud behind it.

It pulled up next to the three vehicles that were already in the lot in front of the covered porch. Jay sat up taller next to Felicity, and she stroked the top of his head to comfort him at the surprise.

A tall, handsome gentleman in sunglasses stepped out of the vehicle, his longish brown hair had a bit of a stylistic wave to it, and the cowlick at the front made him look boyish. His tie was pulled down and the top button of his shirt was open. In three long strides, he was up on the porch, pulling his sunglasses off. His face was contorted with worry as he grabbed the lawyer by the shoulders. "Lucian, tell me it's not true. This has to be a nightmare. Where is Lizzy right now?"

Mr. Wright took hold of the man's shoulders and shook his head. "I'm sorry to say it, Heath, but it's true. Elizabeth is already at the funeral home. Her daughter here identified and released the body."

Heath froze for half a second, his brows knitting together as he turned toward Felicity and Darren. "Daughter?"

The lawyer gestured toward her. "Yes, this is Felicity Stilton, Elizabeth's daughter, and Detective Willis from the Redwood Cove Police Department. Felicity, this is Heath Anderson, the vineyard's vice president."

Felicity stood up slightly and nodded to him

while the man took hold of Darren's hand and shook it. She was struck by how young and handsome the vineyard's vice president was. He couldn't have been more than thirty, but he seemed to know her mother intimately enough to call her Lizzy. She knew that Liz hated when people called her that, even though she knew little else about her mother.

Heath offered Felicity a wide smile and took her hand to shake as well. "It's a pleasure to meet Lizzy's daughter."

His green eyes sparkled, and when he took her hand, a bit of electricity went up her arm, and her heart rate sped up a little. A blush reached her cheeks and she found herself smiling awkwardly and looking away. Her gaze landed upon Mr. Wright's.

The smile that didn't leave his lips once the whole time that they'd been there widened just a little. "Are you finished with the paperwork, Miss Stilton?"

She nodded quickly, gathered up the papers, and handed them back to the lawyer along with his pen. "Of course."

"It was a pleasure meeting you both. Heath, Darren, Felicity. If you have any questions or I can assist in any way, feel free to call me. Otherwise, my wife just texted me. I'm late coming home for dinner." He chuckled and started toward the late model sedan.

It pained Felicity to see the man go. She wanted to ask a million questions, but not one of them would form enough in her mind to come out on her tongue. They were like wisps of smoke in her mind. If she tried to grasp one, it would disappear.

HEATH TOOK a seat at the table with Darren and Felicity. Felicity sat back down, and Darren sat down with her. She needed his support, and he was going to give it.

The vice president's smile returned, and then his gaze slipped over toward Darren. "So, you're the detective on this case?"

Darren couldn't have sat up straighter if he'd tried. Even though the man across the table slouched in his seat, Darren's senses were telling him he needed to be careful with how he answered each and every question. In fact, it would have been better if he could turn things around and ask a few questions of his own. "That's correct. The lawyer said that you were on a business trip. Where were you last night? This morning?"

He blinked, but his smile didn't falter at all. "Napa Valley. There's a winery convention going on there. Lizzy was supposed to go, but she came down with a cold, so I went alone."

Darren nodded. "And there are plenty of witnesses to attest to this."

"Of course." That smile didn't falter, but Heath's eyes narrowed just a bit. "Am I a suspect in a murder case, Detective? I thought Lucian said that Lizzy had taken her own life?"

"On first glance, that's what it appears to be, but the case isn't closed just yet."

Felicity glanced Darren's way with confusion flickering across her face. Darren could have kicked himself. Sure, he was just pressing this man's buttons in a show of police dominance, but he hadn't thought how his words would affect the girl next to him.

He rested a hand on her shoulder. "What would you like to do now, Felicity? Would you like me to take you home?"

Her worried eyes searched his for a moment, the blue in them seeming to deepen in the fast fading light. "I'd like to go up to the main house, if

I'm allowed? But I hate to tie you up since you gave me a ride here."

"I can drive you home if you'd like," Heath said, jumping in before Darren could answer.

Felicity looked back toward the vice president with surprise, "Oh, I really don't want to put anyone out. I hate causing trouble."

Darren shook his head at the man and squeezed his hand that still rested on her shoulder. "It's no trouble at all. I don't mind staying with you as long as you need."

A smile spread across her lips when her gaze met his again. "I'd appreciate it if you did."

Warmth spread through his chest. Her vulnerability was evident in her expression, as well as relief because of his offer. He was suddenly tempted to hug her. The poor girl had a lot going on, several surprises that could put anyone into a shocked state, but she was handling it all well. He squeezed her shoulder lightly again and stood. "Let's go ahead and get started toward the house."

Darren couldn't see mirth in Heath Anderson's smile, but still it didn't falter. The man's eyes remained on Felicity, and he stood when she did. He bowed slightly toward her, and then scratched his head, looking up at her between his lashes in a boyish manner. "I may as well tell you now, because you'll find out as soon as you head up to the main house. Lizzy and I were in a relationship. We ended it last week, but several of my things are up at the house that might clue you in on that, and I didn't want things to get awkward between us."

The news didn't surprise Darren at all. The vice president of the vineyard was much too relaxed and seemed to treat the place as though he'd owned it himself. Darren narrowed his eyes at him.

"Oh," Felicity said, blushing a bit and breaking eye contact with the vice president. The news didn't appear to be a complete surprise to her. "That's really none of my business. I wouldn't judge you or let things get awkward because of that."

Mr. Anderson stepped forward and grabbed her hand in both of his.

Her blush deepened.

Darren's hand slipped toward his gun, but he stopped before it reached the handle. What? Was he going to shoot the guy for touching Felicity? He was being ridiculously overprotective. Why did this situation bring those feelings out in him? He wasn't normally so touchy.

The man smiled wider, his eyes sparkling in the recessed porch lights. "I'm so glad to hear it. I really hope that we can become friends. You can feel free to ask me anything and let me help you in any way as you take over your mother's position at the vineyard."

She blinked and shook her head, the coloring leaching from her cheeks. The girl's every emotion seemed to display like a neon sign on her face. "I don't know about that. I have a job already. I'm just here to settle things in the fairest way possible."

"Oh." Heath's brows knitted with exaggerated worry. "I do hope you won't sell the vineyard, I'd hate to see the many employees here get laid off because of new management."

She swallowed, her eyes growing wider for a moment. "Oh no. I wouldn't want that either. I will try to find the fairest solution for everyone. You can trust me on that."

His smile returned, and he leaned forward, pulling her hand to his lips. "Just like your mother," he said, and then squeezed her hands openly, seemingly oblivious to Darren's glare.

Darren didn't like the effect that the vice president had on Felicity. She seemed to react to his every whim, and he played her almost like a puppet. He was too charismatic. Is this how he got to her mother as well? He certainly was a smooth operator. Darren slipped an arm slightly around Felicity's shoulders, and they both turned together toward the path that led to the main house. Her golden retriever ran a few feet ahead of her, tugging playfully at the end of the leash.

The warmth of her skin under his fingertips sent a little tingle up his arm. He smiled at himself and then frowned. This wasn't good. He was getting close to having feelings for this woman ... but maybe it was just because he knew her from his past. She was in a vulnerable state and needed someone to rely upon. He would do his best to help her tonight, but then close the case and put distance between them in the morning.

Nodding slightly, he decided that truly was the best course of action. It was his first case, and he couldn't go falling for the victim's daughter.

Chapter Four

FELICITY HAD NEVER BEEN inside Liz's home. She used the keys that were with her mother's personal effects. As she walked through the immaculate living room, she was struck by the scents of vanilla and lavender—the same smell that she remembered Liz always wafting when they walked together. Nothing in the house seemed out of place. The pictures above the mantel were of Liz on vacation in several exotic places. A couple of them had Heath in them with her. Not one picture was of Felicity, but then, Liz hadn't ever asked for a picture, and Felicity hadn't thought to even offer one. And as far as she could tell, Liz didn't have one thing in the house that showed she even had a daughter at all.

Darren had trailed behind her several feet, allowing her space to visit her mother's things without feeling crowded or rushed. She appreciated that about him. On the outside, the house appeared to be a common farmhouse, but inside the furnishings were much more modern and conservative than the country feel one would have expected. The couches were brown leather, and the coffee table was made of glass with an antler base. Artwork and vases decorated the walls and tops of the stands.

They meandered into the kitchen. Felicity took a deep breath, turning back toward Darren. "So, this is where they found her?"

He nodded. "Today was the new housekeeper's first day at work. She found the body and called 9-1-1."

A half-laugh escaped her. "She probably quit after that."

"Probably." He shrugged.

Sitting on the table were a few pill bottles and a bottle of cough medicine. "So, you think this was a suicide because of the pills? But Heath said something about Liz having a cold, right? Could it possibly have been a medicine interaction?"

"That is still a possibility, but the sleeping pill bottle she still had in her grasp was empty. It appeared she'd taken many of them. Also, she'd left a note."

Felicity blinked. "What did it say?"

He frowned at her a moment, as if unsure he wanted to tell her.

She held the back of the chair she stood next to. "I'm fine. I can handle it."

"It's hard being lonely. I don't think I can take it anymore."

Tears welled in her eyes. Liz had lived alone for so long, but when would anyone get used to living alone? And didn't Heath say something about having broken up with her? Her heart ached in her chest. Maybe if she'd reached out to Liz a little more… Maybe if Felicity had tried a little harder to make the relationship between the two of them happen… Maybe she could have done something to have kept Liz from feeling so lonely—so alone.

Warm hands gripped her shoulders and pulled her into a hug. Her cheek rubbed against the soft cotton of Darren's button-down shirt. She took a deep breath and drew in his clean, manly scent. Tears flowed more easily now that he had his arms wrapped around her. She folded her arms around his back and leaned into him. He patted her on the shoulder. "It's not your fault. I know you think it might be. I know you're thinking about all the things you could have done differently to stop her. But you can't blame yourself for someone else's decisions."

His voice vibrated in his chest, and even that feeling soothed her. Behind her, Jay yipped. He was always sensitive to her emotional states. After closing her eyes and taking in another breath of Darren's scent, she pulled away and swiped the wetness from her cheeks. "You're right. I understand that, but it still hurts to think that I could've—"

"They all think that. Every family that's ever lost a loved one to suicide. They all think they could have done something differently that would have stopped it. But depression is a mental health issue. If your mother wasn't getting the help she needed from a professional, nothing you could have done would have stopped this from happening."

"I have a master's degree in psychology, Darren." She frowned up at him. "I could have been the professional that helped her. That saw this coming and pointed her the right direction."

He frowned back at her. "It doesn't matter. Everyone has a blind spot when it comes to family. You make excuses for behavior. You fail to see flaws and signs. It's normal. And sometimes people put on even more of a front with family to convince their family that everything is okay. It's the reason physicians shouldn't treat their family members."

She had no answer for that. He was right. It's possible that signs were there, even in their brief meetings, but she'd chosen to ignore them. Liz could have been great at keeping up a façade. Maybe that's why things were always so perfect about her appearance… about her house. Felicity took a deep breath and let it out slowly. "Okay. You're right."

"Good. Don't beat yourself up about this, okay?"

Her eyes met his and he smiled down at her, the dimple playing hide and seek in his cheek. What would she have done if Darren hadn't offered to come with her? Could she have really handled all this alone? Even though she hadn't seen him in over eight years, she felt comfortable around him, like they truly were old friends and not just acquaintances. "Okay. I won't."

His smile widened.

"I'm going to head upstairs," she said, pointing toward the staircase.

"Do you want me to come with you?"

She shrugged. "It's okay if I go up alone."

"As long as you don't have a pity party…"

Really? She huffed. "I won't."

"If I hear any sobbing, I'm going to come right up."

She rolled her eyes. "What? Are you my older brother now?"

He shrugged. "Maybe."

The short banter made her laugh, and she realized that was what Darren was going for. She shook her head at him and started up the stairs, Jay following right behind her. Upstairs there were only three bedrooms. One of them had been converted into a home gym with a treadmill, a spin cycle, and a flat screen TV mounted on the wall. The guest room was tidy and small and hadn't appeared to have been touched in quite a while. When she reached the master bedroom, the scent of rosemary grew stronger and the vanilla became fainter. The same shades of brown dominated her bedroom, with dark wood furniture and a beige suede comforter. But the bed was unmade, and several outfits of clothes were thrown on the back of the chair at her vanity.

A suitcase lay opened on the floor next to the dresser, where several of the drawers had been left open with the contents of the drawers hanging half out of them. Felicity blinked in surprise at the state of the room. Everything about Liz was immaculate and perfect, but her bedroom was a mess. Maybe Darren had been right. Liz appeared practically perfect outwardly, where the rest of the world could see her, but in private, she was messy. Maybe this bedroom showed what her mother's internal state was actually like. Her bedroom made her look more human to Felicity than Liz had ever seemed before.

Felicity took a deep breath and sat on the bed. She really took in the environment of her mother's inner sanctum. Next to her mother's bed, on the nightstand, was a turned over picture frame. Felicity picked it up and peered at another picture of Liz and Heath together. This time they were on a tropical beach, and on the bottom a printed banner read "Merry Christmas." The date on the photo said it was from last year. Maybe this was the reason Liz always declined when Felicity invited her to family gatherings over the holidays. It seemed Liz had plans of her own.

Her messy bun felt loose, and Felicity took out her tie-band and decided to do her pony tail again, even though she needed to wrap the tie one extra time around her blonde hair in order to make it work. It felt a little tight, but it was better than the bun that had been falling out. The action of doing her hair made her look down, and she spied something between the nightstand and the bed that shined in the light. Curious, she pushed the comforter out of the way and found a notebook that had fallen in the crack. The leather-bound notebook was kept closed by an elastic band, which Felicity pulled to the side.

Inside she found dates, notes, and journal entries. She flipped through the book and found that the entries had started last spring and went through half of the notebook. Liz had taken note of things she was thankful for, goals she wanted to meet, and goals she had met.

Felicity closed the notebook. This felt so personal, like she was truly looking into her birth mother's brain. It could help her understand her mother a bit more, get a little closer to her, and maybe even figure out the question that was eating her up ever since she'd found out Liz had taken her own life. Why?

After spending a little more time looking through some of Liz's things, she glanced at the time on the alarm clock. With surprise, she discovered she'd been upstairs for nearly an hour. Jay's collar jingled against the hardwood floor as he looked up at her. "You ready to go home?"

He leapt to his feet. She smiled down at him. Together they headed for the stairway, the journal in Felicity's hand. When she reached the living room area, she found Darren sitting on the couch, looking down at his phone. He looked up at her as she came in the doorway. "Sorry for taking so long."

Shaking his head, he stood and put his phone in his back pocket. "No worries. You seem to be doing okay. Find something?" he asked, gesturing at the notebook in her hands.

"Yep. It's Liz's journal."

"That's great. I hope that you find some closure in there."

Felicity's heart ached in her chest. "Me too. But it's getting late. You want to grab a bite to eat on the way home? My treat."

He lifted a brow. "What if I want to eat at La Pierre's?"

She laughed. "If La Pierre's is open and it's what you really want."

"Only if La Pierre's has a good burger. That's what I'm in the mood for."

"Oh, man. I could really use a milkshake too."

He laughed. "Let's do it."

DARREN GUIDED Felicity back down the path through the field on the way to the wine store where his car was parked. JJ ran ahead, off the leash. Part of Darren wished he could have the kind of freedom and joy only ever found in a dog running loose.

"Wow." Felicity stopped suddenly, making him almost run into her.

He shot a glance toward her and found her looking upward. His gaze followed hers, and he found the most beautiful skyscape he'd ever seen. His heart leapt in his chest. The winery was only a little outside of the town limits, but it was enough that the absence of the glare of the lights from the city allowed the night sky to shine through. With just an open, moonless sky, and no buildings blocking the way, it felt like they could see almost every star in the Milky Way. "Wow is right."

Felicity's eyes were filled with wonder as she focused on the stars overhead. Darren couldn't help but slip his gaze toward her. She'd changed her hairstyle when she was upstairs, and now that she had it in a ponytail, she really looked much more like the freshman girl who'd been over to his house a few times right before he graduated high school. He vividly remembered her. She was shy and quiet but would occasionally say something surprisingly snarky. If she hadn't been like that, would he even have remembered her?

They continued walking, but it was hard to keep their eyes focused on the dark path in front of them, or the lights of the wine store up ahead. Still, Darren stayed watchful to allow Felicity the chance to admire the sky.

"Beautiful night, isn't it?" Heath Anderson leaned against a post on the covered porch at the wine store.

Felicity tripped a little when he spoke because her eyes were still glued to the sky. Darren caught her by the elbow to steady her. She shot a glance toward him with a nod of thanks and then straightened.

"Is the sky always like this out here?" she asked.

Heath nodded. "Pretty much." He rolled a pen between his fingers, letting it move between them in such a smooth and regular motion that it seemed like a frequent habit. "I always told Lizzy that we should consider opening a bed and breakfast out this way, just because of the view, but she was friends with the owner of the one in town and didn't want to take customers away from them."

"The Redwood Cove Inn," Darren added.

"That's the one. But we'd hardly compete with them. They've got the ocean view there, but we'd have this open sky and the vineyards which create a view of their own."

"It really is a gorgeous view on its own." Felicity rubbed her bare arms as the breeze picked up. The sky overhead still had most of her attention.

"Well, we really should be going. It's getting late." Darren opened the back door of his sedan to allow JJ to hop in. The golden retriever happily followed his hand gesture.

Heath pushed off from the post and took a step off the porch. "I'm sorry we didn't get much of a chance to talk, Felicity. I'd love to talk to you some about Lizzy, the winery, and everything else, if we could make the time? I'm happy to help you with making the funeral arrangements or settling the estate. Anything at all, I'm here for you."

Felicity's brow furrowed a little. "Thank you. I have work in the morning, but I'll be back out sometime in the afternoon. I'd be happy to meet with you then."

He rushed forward and grabbed hold of her hand again. Darren ground his back teeth. He didn't like this guy getting so familiar with Felicity so quickly. Heath had touched her more times in their two meetings than Darren had the entire time he'd known the girl. And Felicity didn't seem keen on the frequent contact, either, though she didn't pull her hand away.

"That sounds great. I'll see you tomorrow afternoon." Heath squeezed her hands a bit and then let them go.

Darren opened the passenger door for Felicity, and she offered him a shy half smile as she slid into the seat. He eyed the vineyard vice president and noticed that the man had backed away a bit from the car, but still kept his gaze focused on the girl inside. Darren narrowed his eyes at the man. The pen in Heath's hands had started to go to work again. Was it a nervous habit? Outwardly the man seemed relaxed and welcoming, but that constant movement in his hand made Darren wonder what else the man might have up his sleeve.

When Darren slipped into the driver's seat of the sedan, he glanced over at Felicity, who had a hand covering her mouth as she released a big yawn. He started the car and made sure the heater was turned on low. "It sure got late awful quick. Hopefully we'll find a burger joint on the way that's still open."

She nodded, yawning again, and talking in the half-yawn state. "It's almost nine."

Darren pushed the car into reverse and pulled out of his parking spot. The headlights shined over the man on the porch one last time and exposed an expression that Darren hadn't seen before. For the first time, Heath Anderson wasn't smiling, and his eyes were still focused on Felicity.

Chapter Five

IT WAS NEARLY eleven when Felicity watched Darren drive away from the small ranch home that she rented. A light was on in the master bedroom, letting her know that her roommate, Georgia, was still up. She stepped inside the house and hung Jay's leash on the hook. The golden retriever danced his way inside, happy to be home after the long day.

"Honey, I'm home," Felicity called out.

The master bedroom door sat open, and Georgia stood in the doorway wearing fuzzy pajamas with a brow raised. Her curly red hair was held back by a crystal headband, and her face was unnaturally shiny, from the moisturizing mask she'd applied. Georgia spoke through taut lips, as though any movement might interrupt her mask's effectiveness. "Who was that who dropped you off? Where have you been?"

Felicity sighed. "I forgot to call you after everything happened." She frowned. "Liz is gone. She committed suicide."

Georgia's eyes went wide. "What? Are you serious? Oh, honey!" She rushed forward and pulled Felicity in a tight hug. "That's awful news." She pulled away, looking up into Felicity's face. "Are you okay?"

"I'm sad, but not a wreck, you know? As much as I wanted to get to know Liz, I didn't really know her yet, you know?"

Georgia lifted a brow at her again and put her hands on her hips. Even though she was only five-foot-one, she was all attitude, and honest to a fault. "You know? That's something you say when you're lying to yourself some, Felicity. Like you want me to confirm something that you already know isn't true. That means the truth is, you are a bit of a wreck over it, and you did know her well enough to be a wreck over it."

A frown tugged at Felicity's lips and her eyes welled. She blinked the tears and swiped them with her hand. She shook her head. "Fine. I'm upset about it. I'm even a little mad. I wanted to get to know her, but what I did know about her was that she wasn't very interested in getting to know me. I wanted her to be like a mother should be, but she'd given me up for adoption because she knew that she wasn't capable of it. I'm grateful that she was smart enough to see that in herself. I'm grateful for the parents I have. But I can't help this emptiness in my chest now that I know she's gone and I'll never get the chance to see her become the mother I wanted her to be."

Georgia opened her arms wide and Felicity stepped into them. She hugged her roommate, which could have been awkward since she was nearly six inches taller, but it felt much more comforting than anything else. Georgia had been her roommate since junior year at college. They roomed together while Felicity pursued her master's degree, too. Georgia's degree was in hotel-restaurant management, and she'd gotten a great job managing a high-end seafood restaurant near the marina, which is why they chose this house to share for the proximity. She patted Felicity's back. "Doesn't it feel better to open up about your feelings? You're allowed to have them, you know. Isn't that saying, 'Physician, heal thyself?' You can't just go around helping everyone else and not letting anyone help you. What am I here for otherwise?"

"You're right." Felicity squeezed her roommate, pulled back, and swiped her eyes again. "Thank you for being here for me."

"Of course." Georgia said.

A plastic tub banged against the wall of the kitchen as Jay came through the narrow doorway with his dog food dish in his mouth. Felicity blinked at him in surprise. He hadn't done that since he was a puppy. She laughed. "I guess someone's hungry for real food. Half my burger wasn't enough for you, huh?"

She stepped toward him and pulled the dish from his mouth.

"Let me go pull this mask off and we'll sit down and talk as much as you need." Georgia started toward her bedroom again.

Felicity stopped with the feed bowl in her hand. "No. I'm fine. Really, I am. It's late and you're tired. And I'm just going to feed Jay and then head to bed myself. It's been a long day."

She eyed her for a moment and then shrugged.

"If you say so. But if you change your mind, wake me up. I'm here for you, babe."

Everything her roommate said put a smile on Felicity's face. She nodded to her and then headed into the kitchen where she put a scoop of dog food in Jay's bowl and set it at her feet by the kitchen table as she sat down. Then she opened the journal and decided to read a few pages while Jay was eating.

DARREN HAD NEVER BEEN one for taking the elevator in order to just go up to the second floor of his apartment building, but because it had gotten so late, he half considered it when he passed the bay of doors. Out of habit, though, he continued to the stairwell.

His cell phone notified him of a text message as he spilled out onto the hallway of the second floor. He checked his message and found that it was from his youngest brother, Tony.

Need money for food.

Darren frowned at the message. His thumbs worked across the small keyboard on his smart phone. *Really? You starving to death?*

Yessss. Only eating ramen is hard. Haven't eaten in forever.

Don't you have a meal card for the cafeteria? Darren's brother was nineteen and a sophomore at UCLA.

But dinner was like five hours ago and some friends want to go out. Come on, bro, just twenty bucks?

Darren rolled his eyes. *Fine, but not a penny more until you visit dad. Got it?*

Got it :)

He'd always been closest to his younger brother. He rarely talked to Kent, since Kent was busy being a husband and father. But they all stayed in touch with their father as much as they could since their step-mother passed away two years ago.

As Darren stood in front of his apartment door, he pulled up his bank on his smartphone and made a quick transfer to his brother's account. Then he slipped his phone in his pocket and unlocked the door. The darkness in the room felt especially heavy and oppressive today. It wasn't like he hadn't been living alone in this same apartment for the past three years. Darkness was the absence of light. And today he'd spent the whole afternoon with a surprising source of brightness: Felicity.

A lamp sat on the side table next to his hunter green sofa, and he felt for the switch in the dark.

After clicking it on, he collapsed into the faux suede seat. He normally would have been home hours before. Maybe he would have stopped for a burger on the way home like he had with Felicity. Thinking of her now, while he sat on his couch, warmed his heart in an unexpected way. She hadn't changed much since high school. Snarky, clever, with a pretty smile. But he liked her better now. Maturity had made her more confident, and nothing was more beautiful than a woman who knew who she was.

It was unfortunate that they had to meet again under these less-than-ideal circumstances. He closed his eyes for a moment and sunk into the sofa a bit, letting the muscles in his neck and shoulders relax for a moment. A frown tugged at his lips. He didn't want to fall asleep on the couch, but if he stayed like he was for very long, that was exactly what he was going to do. Steeling himself, he opened his eyes, stood, and started for the bathroom. He had that sticky feeling on his back, under his shirt, from sitting in the car for most of the day.

The ringtone on his phone went off. He shook his head. An unrecognized number flashed on the screen of his phone. Did Tony already blow through that twenty? Was he calling from a friend's phone? Darren sighed. He needed to make sure he stood firm and not give into his kid brother's every whim, no matter how badly he wanted to spoil him. He prepared himself for the inevitable argument and was ready to stand his ground.

"Hello," he said in a grumpy tone as he flicked on the overhead light in his bathroom.

"Um, hi. Darren?" a female voice asked with hesitation.

The sound of her voice sent a chill through him, and he stopped dead, facing the mirror in the bathroom. His maple brown eyes had widened a bit as his heart picked up speed. "Felicity?"

"Yeah, it's me. I'm sorry to bother you when you only left like forty-five minutes ago, but I've been reading through the last couple entries in Liz's diary, and even the one she made last night. She really doesn't seem depressed at all about her break up with Heath, as the suicide note suggests. In fact, it seems, according to this, that she was the one who broke up with him, possibly."

"Hmmm. It's not unusual for anyone to lie to themselves over a break-up situation. Maybe she was trying to make her feel better by fooling herself. People do that." He didn't want to discourage her completely, but it certainly wasn't enough evidence to discredit the suicide note.

"That might be true, but the journal goes on to talk about plans she has for the next week or two… even on to the next month," she said quickly as though afraid he'd try to discredit her before she could even finish.

He took a deep breath when she was done. The last thing he wanted to do in this situation was play devil's advocate, but as a detective he needed to stick with the facts and not let hunches or emotions dictate the truth. "Even people who deal with depression put things into their calendar they intend to do in the future when they are up. They throw all those things away and forget about them when they are down."

She chuckled a little to herself. "I guess you're right. It's just that my gut tells me that Liz wouldn't do this to herself. In no way did she seem depressed or unstable in any of the times we spent together. I can't believe she'd put herself into that kind of place emotionally over a break-up."

"It's okay to feel that way. As family, it's perfectly normal to look for evidence to the contrary. But I'll tell you what. The points you're making are valid, but not enough to refute the evidence we have that point in the direction of suicide. Keep digging. It can't hurt as long as you don't let yourself get too obsessed and you still listen to reason, and it seems like you're still willing to listen. I'll keep the case open all day tomorrow. If you find more evidence, let me know. I'm willing to listen."

It was her turn to take a deep breath. "Darren, I'm so glad that it was you who was assigned to this case and broke the news to me. I don't know what I would have done all day without your help."

"Are you getting sappy on me now?" He laughed to break the tension.

"Maybe just a little. A girl is allowed to get sappy now and then, right?" She laughed back, and it hit all the right musical notes to send a thrill through his chest.

He frowned. He couldn't be falling for this girl already.

"Anyway. Thank you for listening to a crazy chick like me get a little irrational, blow things up out of proportion a bit, and even get a little sappy."

"No problem. Try to get some sleep tonight. Don't stay up all night reading that journal."

She sucked in a breath. "How'd you know?"

"Maybe you're a little bit predictable?"

A gasp rang in his ear. "No way. I'm going to

have to work harder. A girl is supposed to have a little mystery."

"Don't forget I'm a detective. You'll need more than a little mystery to keep me interested." He was flirting. What was he doing?

"I'll remember that. And I'm closing this book right now and heading to bed. Have a good night, detective." She had a little lilt to her voice that made him smile.

"Goodnight, Felicity." His voice grew husky when he said her name. Suddenly he was really liking saying it. He hung up the phone before things could get any sappier than they had.

He eyed himself in the mirror again, blinking hard and running his hands through his hair. There was no doubt about it. Felicity Stilton was having an effect on him. She was more than just the family of a victim in his case. She was more than just a childhood friend he was getting reacquainted with. The banter that they'd shared throughout the day and even while they were getting their burgers felt natural. It felt right. It felt like the piece to the puzzle of his life that he didn't even know had been missing. He wanted to spend more time with her, but at the same time he was afraid of his growing affection for her.

The screen on his smartphone had gone dark, and he lifted it, pushing the home button. Then he went to his last phone call and added her name to the number, so it wouldn't come up unknown again. His heart squeezed in his chest. Hope. Hope grew like a balloon in his chest, making little room for anything else, pushing his heart and affecting it as well. He hoped she'd call again. He wanted her to —but didn't want her to.

He'd just gotten the new position of detective. Things were looking up for his career. He'd been saving up for a down payment on a house that he could then move into with his dad. It would be the start of life outside of apartments and paying rent. They could get a yard and maybe even a dog, like the one Felicity had.

With a shake of his head, he turned on the hot water faucet. Even when thinking about his goals for the future, she was worming her way into his thoughts. He needed to get back on track. He wasn't ready for a relationship. They were too difficult, and he had too many responsibilities. Too much baggage. Why would any girl want to come in on the middle of that?

He blew out a breath and pulled his shirt over his head. It was time to focus on his own life and push aside any thoughts of banter and flirting. He set his phone on the counter next to the sink. Besides, she'd probably have no reason to call him again anyway. After another deep breath, he hopped into the shower.

Chapter Six

FELICITY LIED. Though not because she'd wanted to. Sleep avoided her, and she tossed and turned for over an hour before giving up and picking up the journal to read more. Although she could find no definitive proof that her birthmother didn't take her own life, her gut feeling had become much stronger that the journal was written by a hopeful, all business Liz—the same strong woman she'd met on several occasions who never seemed to have a hint of manic or depressive behaviors.

By five-thirty a.m., however, she was utterly exhausted, and her vision had gotten a bit blurry from the strain on her eyes. She shut off the bedside lamp in her room, though the faintest bit of gray glow seeped through the blinds on her north-facing window as the sun rose in the east. She sighed and picked up her phone to shoot a text message to her boss, the vice principal. Her teeth ached from gritting them so hard while she typed.

She needed a sick day, though. Not only because she couldn't possibly get up in an hour and get ready for work, but also because Darren had promised her one day only to find evidence that Liz's death was something other than suicide. If it wasn't suicide, and it was just an accident, it would rest easier on Felicity's mind and soul. If it was neither suicide nor an accident, and there was foul play involved, she needed proof so that Darren could take the investigation more seriously.

All in all, she honestly hoped it was just an accident. Maybe Liz's cold medication interacted with her sleeping aid? Maybe she ended up taking too much sleeping aid because she'd thought she hadn't taken it yet. But that didn't make sense with the suicide note. If it had been just an accident, she wouldn't have left a note. And if it wasn't suicide or an accident, then someone else wrote that note. The thought of it gave her a shiver, and she pulled her blanket up higher on her shoulder as she settled into her bedding, her back facing the window.

"Hey, sleepyhead. Get up," Georgia said in a singsong way, shaking Felicity's shoulder."

"Ugh," she moaned. "I called in sick today, let me get a little sleep. Can you get me up at nine?"

Georgia laughed. "Girl, it's ten."

Felicity shot up to a sitting position and picked up her cellphone. It was a few minutes after ten a.m. How could that be possible when it felt like she'd hardly been asleep at all?

Jay sat on the edge of the bed with his chin resting on the mattress, his tail wagging behind him. Felicity met eyes with him, and her irresponsibility made her stomach queasy. "I'm so sorry, boy. You probably need to go outside so badly."

Georgia ran her fingers through the longish hair on the back of Jay's head and neck. "Nah, he's good. I figured you had called in sick since you never sleep in, and no matter if you were close or not, Liz's death is going to affect you. After all, she is your birthmother."

Tears stung the back of Felicity's eyes. "What did I ever do to deserve a friend like you?"

"Not enough, I'm afraid," Georgia said, leaning back with a huge grin on her face. "Because this friend of yours just walked JJ down to *Sweets and Treats*, picked him up some of those vegan doggie biscuits he's so crazy about, and grabbed us one of those giant donuts to share. Now, who do you love?"

"You. Nobody but you, wifey." Felicity's heart swelled in her chest and she pulled her covers off, taking the coffee cup offered by her best friend and roommate.

"Of course it's nobody but me." Georgia lifted a brow and then turned on her heel and headed for the door. "Now get in the kitchen; I'm ready to get started on this donut, aren't you?"

"Yes, girl!" Felicity jumped from her bed and hugged Jay, like she always did in the mornings. "Good morning, sunshine," she said in his ear as she gave him a squeeze. Then she stood and followed her roommate toward the kitchen to enjoy the donut and her coffee.

ONCE FELICITY DROVE up to the winery, she let Jay out of the back of her SUV and commanded, "Stay by."

She hated putting Jay on a leash, and the golden retriever had been trained to walk without one. Jay sat at her heels while she grabbed her messenger bag from the back seat and closed up her vehicle.

"It's great to see you again, Felicity," a deep baritone called to her from the covered porch of the wine store. Heath Anderson stood, leaning against the railing with a smile, wearing a rumpled suit similar to the one he'd worn the night before, but this one was a shade of brownish-gray rather than blue.

"Thanks. I'm going to head up to the house and look around at some of my mother's things." She rarely referred to Liz as her mother, but for some reason she felt the need to convey that so that no one questioned her motives. She wasn't ready to share her thoughts on what she thought about Liz's death with anyone yet. Heath was, after all, the vice president of the vineyard and Liz's ex-boyfriend. He'd likely have motive to kill Liz.

Felicity frowned at herself as she turned up the walkway with Jay. She didn't like to think of people she'd met as being potential murderers. That thought was almost as hard for her to believe that Liz took her own life. When she got up to the house, she went to put the key in the door, but found it unlocked.

With a frown, she opened the door and called inside, "Hello?"

Clattering noises came from the kitchen, and

then a young Asian woman poked her head out from the doorway, her hands covered in rubber gloves and hair pinned back in a bun. She bowed slightly. "Hello."

Jay started trotting her direction, tail wagging in greeting. "JJ, stay by."

The golden stopped in his tracks and sat where he was, halfway between Felicity and the woman from the kitchen. Felicity would have guessed the woman at about the same age as herself. "Hello, can I ask what you're doing?"

Even though the woman's accent was thick and her English, broken, she was easy enough to understand. "I clean. Start with kitchen."

Felicity always had much respect for people who could speak more than one language, even if they didn't speak the other one perfectly. After taking four years of Spanish in high school, she didn't think she could even do as well as this woman did with English. "Are you the housekeeper?"

"Yes." The woman nodded vigorously.

Felicity frowned. Didn't Darren say that the woman had just started the job yesterday, and even found Liz's body on her first day? How traumatic that must have been for her. Felicity drew a few steps closer, standing next to Jay, who obediently stayed seated on the hardwood floor, next to the couch. Then she remembered why she'd come to the house in the first place, and her heart sunk. How would she possibly find any clues at all if the woman had been cleaning this whole time? She used as many gestures as possible while she spoke in the hopes that the woman would understand her. "What time did you come in to clean? Did you start with the kitchen?"

The woman looked toward the ceiling, thoughtful for a moment before lowering her gaze and nodding. "I start at ten. I clean upstairs first."

Disappointment flooded her. It was just after one p.m. There was no way that this woman could clean so poorly that she'd leave clues behind. Although Darren had left the case open, he hadn't made the scene secure so that no one would mess with it. Now it had been thoroughly changed. She collapsed onto the couch arm in disappointment.

"Mr. Page say it's okay to clean." The woman frowned when she saw Felicity's expression and pulled her gloves from her hands.

"Mr. Page?" Felicity asked, remembering the tall sour man she'd met the afternoon before. Now that was one man she might believe actually capable of murder. In fact, had he asked her to clean the scene to obscure any evidence of his wrongdoing?

The woman nodded enthusiastically, saying something under her breath in a language Felicity didn't understand.

Felicity shook her head. She needed to think clearly. What other clues might there be of foul play? Just then footsteps stomped on the porch outside. She looked up in the direction of the afternoon sun and found Mr. Anderson coming in through the screen door.

He smiled and knocked on the open doorway. "Hello, again. I thought I'd come up and see if there's anything I can do to help." He bowed slightly in the direction of the housekeeper.

Handsome and polite. Her heart fluttered at the thought.

"It seems you've met Miss Kim. She's Mrs. Park's replacement."

"Oh?" Felicity wondered. "So, Liz had a housekeeper before Miss Kim?"

He nodded, drawing closer to her and sitting on the arm of the chair across from her. "Yes, but it seemed Mrs. Park had sticky fingers. Some of Liz's things went missing over the past few months. At first it seemed like she'd misplaced and lost things, but when it seemed much too obvious to be anything other than theft, she fired the woman. Because Liz had no actual proof, she did it discreetly and didn't get the police involved."

Felicity's eyes widened. A thief under Liz's nose? And she fired the woman not very long ago if it was Miss Kim's first day yesterday. "When did all this happen?"

With a half shrug, Heath answered, "Last week?"

A sigh escaped her lips as she watched Miss Kim bow slightly and head back into the kitchen. Cleaning noises continued. Felicity frowned. "A lot happened last week then in Liz's life."

"For sure. That much stuff can really affect a person who was prone to depression, like Liz was."

A frown tugged at Felicity's lip. "Was she seeing anyone for her depression? On medication?"

He shook his head, the wrinkles in his forehead deepening. "No, your mother wasn't diagnosed with depression, but she battled with it often enough. The winery was a stressful business. If I'd known all this stuff would be too much for her, maybe I could have stayed with her. It's shameful that I abandoned her… maybe I could have—"

Felicity shook her head. "No. You can't blame

yourself. You can't burden yourself that way. Liz made her own choices, and who's to say that anything you did could have stopped her from doing what she did?"

For a moment, she felt that she sounded like Darren, and her heart fluttered at the thought. But Darren had been right, and that was why his words slipped past her lips. Her heart felt burdened by the sad expression on Heath's face.

He looked up at her, eyes watery. "Thank you for saying so, but I still feel guilty. I know it's not entirely my fault, and I felt like our breakup was somewhat mutual. We promised to remain friends and business colleagues."

"That's good. Very adult, too." She'd read something similar in Liz's journal.

"I just didn't realize how lonely Liz had gotten, and how much the stress of running this place, firing Mrs. Park, and everything else was affecting her."

"You're talking yourself in a loop of destruction now. Your guilt won't subside until you accept that these changes in her life were inevitable and it's impossible to change the past, no matter how much we'd like to."

He lifted a brow. "That sounded a bit professional. What do you do for a living?"

A blush rose to Felicity's cheeks. "I work in Educational Psychology, helping children with reading disabilities."

He snapped his fingers and nodded. "I knew it had to be psychology or psychiatry. The advice you gave was just too professional."

The blush ran down the back of her neck. "I guess so."

After clapping his hands together and standing, he said, "Anyway. What can I do to help you? I'm willing to do my part in helping you settle the estate and get the winery going in the best possible direction as fast as possible."

She frowned. Honestly, she had no idea where to start in that direction. For a moment, she wondered if he could help her with looking for clues. No one alive probably knew the house better than he did, or her things. But she threw out that idea immediately. She didn't want someone else to tell her she was crazy or trying too hard to see clues where there weren't any. She decided to conjure an excuse. "Actually, I'm here to just process everything personally. I didn't know Liz very well, even though she was my birthmother. I'd like to just spend a day getting to know her through her things."

His eyes went a little wide, and he nodded, offering a knowing smile. "Of course. That makes sense. I don't want to intrude on your private moment." He pulled out his phone. "But let's exchange contact information, if you don't mind. This way you can call me if you need anything at all. I don't usually answer unknown phone numbers, I'm afraid. I really hate spam."

Felicity laughed a little with him as he chuckled. He was right. She rarely answered unknown numbers for the same reason. They exchanged contact information, and then he left quietly. She took a deep breath as she watched him step off the porch and onto the path between the house and the wine shop. Several cars were now parked in the little lot, and an employee in a purple polo shirt led the group for a tasting on the covered porch.

"Excuse me," a small voice said behind her in a thick accent.

Felicity turned around and met eyes with the woman, offering her a small smile. "Yes, Miss Kim?"

The woman's eyes shot toward the doorway where Heath had just left, and then her gaze slipped past Felicity's before pointing at the ground between them. "I sorry I heard what the Mister say." Her gaze came back up to meet Felicity's and she shook her head. "No. Mrs. Park... She no take anything. She not a thief."

Felicity blinked at the woman. The housekeeper certainly understood English much better than she spoke it at least. That was fairly normal as well for people who have at least a cursory knowledge of two languages. She smiled down at the woman. Even though she was only five feet six inches, Miss Kim couldn't have been any taller than her roommate, Georgia. "Okay, I'm not sure what's going on here. I just got here yesterday and only heard about that situation just now. I'm not accusing anyone of stealing, and won't take someone else's word on the matter, understand?"

Her eyes narrowed at Felicity a moment, but then her expression softened. She nodded slowly. "Mrs. Park no stealing."

"Okay, I understand." Felicity nodded. Trying to get the housekeeper to understand that it was none of her business seemed futile. It was best to patronize her a little and placate her. Then Felicity eyed the woman as she went back into the kitchen to resume her work.

Heath had told her that the former maid had been stealing, but it seemed that the new maid and the former maid had some sort of relationship with each other, as it seemed Miss Kim knew Mrs. Park well enough to stand up for her when someone insulted the woman. Fair enough.

Jay lay on the hardwood floor, half on the carpeting between the coffee table and the sofa. The position he slept in showed he wasn't much worried about all the humans had to talk about in this situation. Felicity sighed and looked around. It seemed that the winery was doing well enough that Liz could afford a maid anyway. But was it possible the place had invisible debt. One of the reasons people Liz's age took their own life was due to debts and failing business. She decided to head up to the nook in Liz's bedroom where she had a dark wood desk and a laptop laying on the top of it.

The golden followed her up the stairs and into Liz's room. When she sat in the chair at Liz's desk, Jay plopped down on top of Felicity's feet. She scratched him a bit behind the ears. Having Jay in her life made sure that she rarely, if ever, felt lonely. The warmth of his body on her feet comforted her from the slight draft that came into the room.

She opened the silver and white laptop, listening

to the start-up sequence music as the laptop fired up. Once the lock screen popped up, it asked for a password. Felicity frowned. How on Earth would she figure out what her mother's password had been? No matter what, people tended to be the same when it came to password creation. They used things that they loved in their lives and things that would be easy to remember. But what did Liz love? She thought about the journal written in Liz's words, trying to figure out what she loved and what she might use as a password.

After trying a few things, like Merlot and Chardonnay, Felicity pulled her messenger bag closer to herself and pulled out the leather-bound journal. She flipped through the pages she'd read, looking for words her mother tended to use often and seemed to put special emphasis on.

Even though one word often had flowers and other swirly objects decorating it on every other page, it didn't seem much like Liz to use it as a password. On a whim, Felicity typed it in. Gratitude.

Immediately, the laptop unlocked.

She blinked at the screen. The background of her computer was an aerial picture of the winery, which on the back side went all the way out to cliffs overlooking the ocean. Seemed amazing that a woman who talked a lot about gratitude in her journal and even used it as her laptop password wouldn't be likely to take her own life. None of it made sense to Felicity yet. She started going through the computer, starting with the latest photographs stored in it and moving on to the last documents and spreadsheets that Liz had opened. From what she could see, Dorma Valley Wine had been doing fabulously well and was a success after pulling through some rough times during the last recession. Everything was looking up for the business.

After a few hours of browsing Liz's computer, Felicity leaned back, rolling her head and shoulders to get the tension out. Her stomach growled. She glanced at her smartphone and found that it was already nearly four o'clock. Since the oversized donut that she and Georgia had shared that morning, she hadn't eaten. Jay stood with her as she stretched and closed the laptop. The sun shone brightly through the window. Jay followed her toward the stairs.

As she reached the landing midway down the steps, she noticed Miss Kim heading toward the front door with a few cleaning supplies. Felicity called out to her, "Oh, are you done for the day?"

She nodded and bowed again. "Yeah."

Felicity hopped down the remainder of the steps. "How often do you come to clean the house?"

"Miss Liz say two days a week. Tuesday and Friday. I come yesterday, but no can clean, so I come today." The housekeeper's hands were clasped in front of her; she looked both sad and nervous. "You moving into Miss Liz's house?"

Felicity shook her head. "No, I have a place of my own." She frowned as she drew conclusions. "Does this mean that you won't be needed to clean on Friday this week, since there won't be anyone living here?"

The woman shrugged. "I don' know. Mr. Page say come today. I wait for Mr. Page to tell me."

"Does Mr. Page run the day to day stuff around the winery?"

Miss Kim shook her head and shrugged as though she didn't know.

While she had the woman here, she still wanted to ask her a few questions if she could. "Did anything seem unusual or out of place here as you were cleaning? I know it was your first day, but did you happen to see anything strange?"

Wrinkles appeared in the Asian woman's forehead as she shook her head again. "I don' know."

Felicity's stomach growled again. She hated the idea of raiding Liz's refrigerator, but right now she didn't have much choice. She wanted to keep searching through her mother's things for clues and she didn't have much time left before the "end of the day." If she couldn't find anything substantial, Darren would close the case.

"Is there anything good to eat in the kitchen?" she asked the housekeeper.

Chapter Seven

"HAVE you closed that case yet at the winery?" The police lieutenant sat on the corner of Darren's desk and eyed him with his icy blue glare.

Darren's gaze slipped to the clock on the wall to his right before returning. "There is a bit of circumstantial evidence that there may have been foul play involved. I'm following all the leads."

One of the lieutenant's eyebrows went up his forehead. "Circumstantial evidence, eh? This case shouldn't have been so hard as to take you two days. I'd like to see it closed if things don't become more solid. You have other cases." He tapped at the four other folders sitting on top of Darren's desk.

"Yes, sir." Darren nodded. "I plan to."

The lieutenant ran a hand through his short-cropped graying hair and stood up. "I know you're new at this so I'm trying to be easy-going about it. However, if you drag your feet, the rest of your cases will pile up. Understood?"

Darren nodded again. "Understood, sir."

He blew out a breath as the lieutenant walked toward his office. Darren had been out all day, trying to avoid this conversation. While giving Felicity time to find clues concerning Liz's death, he'd met up with the coroner and found that the tox screen had come back and Liz had over ten sleeping pills in her stomach contents, mixed with both wine and cold medication. The interaction was deadly, but without question, not an accident. Either Liz had tried to kill herself, as the suicide note suggested, or she was murdered—but Darren would need substantial evidence if he was going to upgrade this to a murder investigation.

Although his ringtone was set to silent, he felt it vibrate in his back pocket. He pulled it up and found Felicity's name on the screen. He glanced at the clock again. It was nearly 4:30. She was cutting it close. "Hello, this is Darren Willis."

"Hi Darren, it's Felicity." Her voice had a melodious quality to it, and his body reacted as though shaken by a cold chill.

He frowned. Hadn't he already decided he wasn't going to chase that rabbit down that hole? "So, did you find anything of substance?"

She groaned slightly. "I'm not sure, but I'll tell you what I have found. Just now I opened the fridge and found a roast marinating in it. I talked to the housekeeper, and she said that it seemed like Liz had started the roast marinating yesterday, in the morning."

Darren frowned. "That can't be right. The time of death on the coroner's report is between 8 and 10 a.m. The housekeeper found the body and called it in at 11:20. She'd arrived at the house at 10 a.m., saw Liz's back in the kitchen, called out to her, and then went upstairs to start cleaning. When she came back down about an hour later, she entered the kitchen and discovered the body."

"But the marinade was started yesterday, and the housekeeper said she didn't do it. Who would think to start a marinade and then take their own life? It doesn't make any sense." Her voice had grown a little higher pitched, and she rushed through her words as though afraid Darren might interrupt her.

"I agree with you that it doesn't make sense, but you have to understand something. The coroner's report has ruled this as no accident. If your birth-mother didn't commit suicide, it was murder. And right now, I've got a suicide note. A marinating piece of meat cannot refute that."

Felicity hmphed on the other side of the line. "Is there any chance I could see that note? Is it handwritten?"

"Yes, but it's in my evidence folder. I can't remove it." He peered down at the yellow folder on his desk, opening it past his original report and looking at the rumpled note in the plastic bag.

"Would you be willing to take a picture of it and send it to me?" she asked.

Darren's back teeth tightened. Her request wasn't usual protocol, so he glanced up at the lieutenant's office and saw the man had his back turned. He set his phone up to take a picture of the note and then sent it to Felicity. "Do you have any other evidence? Something more substantial that would say this was a murder?"

Felicity drew in a long breath. "I've been through the financial records on Liz's laptop, and the business was going very well. If she was going to kill herself due to financial reasons, it would have been during the recession when she would struggle through the winter without a paycheck of any kind.

Now wouldn't have been the best time. Also, according to her journal, the break-up was mutual, and Heath confirmed that. Nothing in her writings seemed to suggest that she was especially sad about it."

"You were able to get into her laptop? It was password protected."

"I figured it out. Her password was Gratitude."

Darren's chest tightened. Felicity was making a lot of good points. This didn't seem like such an open and shut case of suicide. Her mother didn't seem to show signs of depression, and though she was on several medications, none of them were for emotional support. The business was doing well, and it seemed the woman had been getting things prepared for dinner only less than two or three hours before taking her own life. It didn't add up, but nothing was substantial enough to provide evidence of murder. "Are you still at the winery?"

"I am."

"Stay there. I'm on my way. I'd like to see what you found on her laptop and maybe question a few people about things. We can't make this a murder case until we have more evidence. I'll be there in about an hour."

"Okay."

He hung up the phone, feeling the tightness in his chest get a little worse. His gut feeling was aligned with Felicity's. Nothing about Liz's suicide case seemed open and shut.

FELICITY TOOK a deep breath as she hung up the phone and bowed slightly to the Asian woman sitting across from her at the kitchen table. "Thank you for your help. I'm sorry I kept you."

"Okay," she said with a smile and stood up. "I go now?"

With a nod, Felicity said, "Yes, and thank you again."

She led the housekeeper to the front door and Jay followed them both. The woman was very humble, bowing again before she left. Felicity watched through the screen door as the woman walked down the path from the house to the wine store. Her stomach grumbled again, and she remembered that she hadn't gotten something to eat yet. With a frown, she peered toward the kitchen. The idea of going back in there and raiding Liz's kitchen was even less appealing this time than it was earlier.

"What do you think, Jay? You want to go down to the wine store and see what they have for sale down there? If I remember right, they make sandwiches, at least."

Jay smiled up at her and wagged his tail.

"I'll take that as a yes." She opened the screen door and let Jay run outside and around the front yard a bit, with his nose to the ground, sniffing. The short bit of freedom was good for a dog who'd been cooped up all afternoon with her, lying on the floor as she searched through Liz's laptop.

A mild breeze blew through, carrying on it a bit of the salty taste of the ocean. She wondered what the scale had been in the aerial photograph. How far exactly was it actually across the vineyards to the cliffs facing the ocean? The blue sky above her had only a smattering of clouds pulled apart in all directions like cotton candy. She walked along the path with her gaze toward the sky again. Somehow the short fields opened up the view to the heavens. The sunsets would be beautiful here. The environment of the vineyard was inspiring, making her almost feel like writing poetry or something. Her heart swelled. If this place had the same effect on Liz, Felicity could add it as one more reason that would make it unlikely that the woman would take her own life.

"I thought I told you to keep that dog on a leash," a harsh, deep voice interrupted her thoughts.

She snapped her gaze from the sky and looked into the narrowed brown eyes of Curtis Page, leaning on the fence right by the gate where the path she was walking led. She blinked at him, her heart lurching in her chest at his icy glare.

"So, you going to put him on a leash or what? We got customers on the tour around through the fields right now, but when they get back for the tasting, the last thing they need is a mutt shoving his nose in their business and jumping all over them."

She blinked at him a few more times, her cheeks heating as anger welled up. "JJ is not a mutt. He's a golden retriever. He's been trained as a therapy dog and would never jump all over a bunch of people. In fact, he's also trained to walk and behave well off-leash."

He rolled his eyes. "It makes no difference; it's still a health code issue. We serve food and wine here. Can't have a dog running around loose, shedding and spreading germs."

Before she knew it, her hands fisted, her fingernails biting into her palms. Her back molars ground against each other, and she was trying to organize her thoughts on how to respond without letting her anger spill over.

"Curtis! She's fine. The dog is very well-behaved. I've witnessed it myself." Heath walked up, smiling at Felicity and then raising a brow at Mr. Page. "Instead of standing there bugging the lovely lady about how she does things on her mother's property, how about you go out to the fields and hunt down the rattlesnake one of the guests claimed they saw on the tour? If you want to know what will ruin a guest's experience faster, a snake bite or a dog hair, I'd be willing to bet it's the former."

"There's more than one snake around here," Curtis mumbled under his breath as he marched away toward the all-terrain vehicle parked nearby. He hopped into the seat of the four-wheeled green and yellow cart-truck and started the engine. He burned out of the parking lot fast enough to throw gravel toward Heath as he peeled away.

Heath jumped to side, frowning at the man in the ATV. "If I didn't know any better, I'd say he did that on purpose."

Jay rushed up to Heath, wagging his tail and putting the top of his head in Heath's hand. Heath smiled down at the golden and pet him. It warmed the ice around Felicity's heart that Curtis Page had left behind and cooled her cheeks. She blew out her cheeks, as though she was pushing the anger out with the air. "It wouldn't surprise me. That man sure is surly."

With a shrug, Heath said, "He's a bit short-tempered and hard to work with. I've told Liz several times that we should replace him."

"Maybe she finally did. It would be motive to kill her, and he seems like the type who would do it." Felicity's heart sunk. Had she just said that out loud?

Heath's eyes widened. "But Liz wasn't murdered, right? It was suicide."

Felicity chewed on her bottom lip, the blood rushing to her cheeks again. How stupid could she be? She spoke poorly about a person she barely knew—her mother would have been mortified. Felicity had been raised to try to understand why people behaved the way they did and help shape people into becoming better. To judge someone based on how they behaved was against everything her mother had taught her. *Hurting people said hurtful things.* She felt ashamed.

And worse, she'd just hinted at the possibility of

murder to Heath. But he seemed trustworthy and was the only person out of town when the murder had happened, right? She pulled in a breath and peered around. "Actually, I don't believe Liz would take her own life. It wasn't like her. I've found a few things that back my theory, and the detective, Darren Willis, is actually coming out to meet me here and see what I've discovered."

He blinked and looked around as Felicity did to make sure no one was around. The wrinkles over his eyebrows deepened. "I really hope you're wrong. I'd hate to think that anyone here would do such a thing. Liz was generally well-liked."

She shrugged. "There's no substantial evidence to it yet, but I found enough for the detective to come out and take a look."

He nodded, leaning back, still looking perturbed by the idea that there might be a murder on the property. And at that moment in time, Felicity's stomach decided to growl again, louder than it had done before. She covered her waist with her arms. He laughed and shook his head. "Was that you?"

"Sorry," she said as she frowned up at him. "I haven't eaten since breakfast. I was heading to the wine store to see if there was something there I could buy."

"Absolutely, I think the staff has already closed up the kitchen, but what would be the point in being vice president of the vineyard if I couldn't at least open the kitchen to make a sandwich." He opened the gate in the fence for her and she let him lead her out. "Do you mind if we keep your dog in the fenced yard of the house? Will he behave? Curtis was right when he said it would be a health code violation to have the dog in the bar."

"Of course! JJ will stay in the yard happily."

Heath's smile widened. "Great."

He led her through the wine store, peering toward the fields. "The tour group will be back shortly, and they will raid the store area for wines, trinkets, and memorabilia, but we shouldn't be disturbed in the kitchen."

"I'm really sorry to impose. I should have brought something to eat instead of trying to bum something from you now." A frown tugged at her lip as she looked up at him.

He smiled down at her, his green eyes sparkling in the low light from the chandelier overhead. A warm hand rested on her shoulder, and he squeezed it slightly. "I'm happy to take care of Liz's daughter in her stead. I'm sure that she wouldn't have wanted you to starve."

They entered the industrial, restaurant-style kitchen. Stainless steel counters, pots, pans, and appliances combined with the white walls and white stone flooring to give the place an immaculate feel. The only splash of color she found was in the red brick oven.

"I'm not much of one for cooking, but we can easily make a few sandwiches. Our chef bakes the bread fresh daily, but always sets a loaf or two to the side at the end of the day for employees to take home. I'll slice up some if you'll head into the cooler and get some meat and toppings?" He gestured in the direction of the large silver door in the wall. "It shouldn't be too hard to find everything we need."

Felicity nodded. "I can do that."

"Great," he said as he grabbed a loaf of bread from the counter and a large bread knife.

The scent of fresh bread still lingered in the air of the kitchen, and Felicity's mouth watered. Her heart fluttered at the idea of finding her own ingredients for the sandwich. She hoped to find an interesting cheese; since it was a winery, she knew they'd have several kinds. She slipped open the silver door. A commotion outside in the bar drew her attention to the bar area. "What was that?"

Heath's brows furrowed as he set down the knife. "Not sure, but I should go check it out. Go ahead and pick out anything you want for the sandwich, and if I'm not back right away, don't wait for me. Eat as much as you want."

"But I need to pay for the sandwich."

He shook his head as he pressed his back against the kitchen door. The most charming smile spread across his lips. "My treat," he said before slipping out the door and not giving Felicity a chance to argue.

She frowned, watching the door swing a bit before settling closed after him. Heath had stopped everything and brought her to the kitchen for a sandwich even though the kitchen staff had already left for the day. He'd already gone above and beyond for her, and now he was going to pay for her sandwich. She'd have to think of a way to pay him back for his kindness.

Cold air seeped toward her from the fridge door that she'd had open a few inches through their conversation. She frowned at herself and slid inside, felt for the light switch, and flicked it on. Then she stepped inside, allowing the door to close behind her since she'd already let too much cold air out.

Meats, cheeses, tomatoes of a few different

kinds spread throughout the cooler, which had to be kept just below freezing. Her breath spread out in a cloud around her and she wrapped her arms around herself for the cold as she quickly chose the items she'd wanted on her sandwich. The cold air blew on her bare arms and the back of her neck from the overhead fan. Once she'd made the best choices, her arms were loaded full. She backed toward the doorway of the refrigerator and pressed on the handle to let herself out, and though the mechanism gave, the door didn't open on first try.

With a frown, she pushed all the items to one arm, so she could try the handle again with her hand. Still, the door didn't budge. She tried again. Nothing. After setting the items in her arms on a nearby wire shelf, she tried with both hands and pushed on the door even harder. The door didn't budge. Dread poured down her spine, adding to the chill she'd already felt. Was she really stuck in the refrigerator?

Chapter Eight

DARREN PULLED over to the side of the narrow driveway on the way to the winery, allowing three cars that were coming from the opposite direction to pass him more comfortably. He lifted his hand in greeting on his steering wheel as the cars passed him, recognizing the purple shirts the employees wore at the winery. He frowned. How many employees would still be around for him to question about the situation now? He peered at his clock. It was a little after six-thirty. He'd told Felicity that he'd be only an hour, but when he'd tried to call her and tell her he was running late, it went to voicemail. He hoped she'd gotten his message.

Once the cars passed him, he resumed his drive up and parked next to one of the only two vehicles in the lot, Felicity's SUV. When he hopped out of his sedan, the jingling of dog tags drew his attention to the wagging tail of JJ, standing with his front paws on the gate. The golden's tongue lolled off to the side, and his whole body wiggled a little back and forth with his tail.

With a smile, Darren stepped over toward the dog and patted him on the head. "Where's your owner, JJ?" He scratched the dog behind the ear. "She can't be too far away, huh?"

After pushing the dog down and back, Darren opened the gate and headed up the long walk to the main house. JJ followed him all the way up to the front porch then barked once at him before running back toward the gate. Darren shook his head at the dog and said under his breath, "I'm not going to be the one to let you out. You'll have to wait for your owner for that."

He frowned at himself. Was he just talking to himself or the dog? He blinked and shrugged. After taking a deep breath, he knocked on the screen door. A few moments passed, and he didn't even hear the slightest movement within. The door was unlocked, so he opened it and stuck his head inside, calling out, "Hello? Felicity?"

Except for the normal hum of household electronics, the house remained silent. Darren stepped in and peered around. He headed for the kitchen, calling out again.

No answer.

He opened the refrigerator and peeked at the marinating roast that sat on the top shelf. When he closed the door, he also noticed a list pinned to the fridge with a magnet. It read like a normal grocery list, nothing special. He glanced down at the kitchen table where Liz's body had been when he first came onto the scene. He recalled the pills and the note that had sat on the table next to her. The coffee cup. Now the table top sat, cleared of all evidence. Felicity had said something about a housekeeper. It's unfortunate they hadn't preserved the scene just a little bit longer. Instead he was having to go by memory. Then something clicked in his head as he stooped down and looked below the table to the floor, playing the scene in his mind. Now that he was thinking about it, there was no pen near the body. If she'd just scribbled a quick note after taking the pills, as the evidence suggested, she wouldn't then get up and put the pen away.

He glanced at the coffee mug that sat on top of the refrigerator loaded with pens and pencils, and a pair of scissors. He pulled an evidence bag out of his pocket and slipped on a rubber glove. It was a long-shot, but it wouldn't hurt to check for prints and partials on the cup and contents. After zipping up the bag, he walked slowly around the room, replaying the previous scene in his mind, using double exposure to lay the one scene overtop of the other.

He kept his glove on as he headed into the living room area and thought things through. Light faded fast as the sun began setting, but he didn't yet want to turn on the lights. When he got to the stairwell, he called upward, "Hello? Felicity?"

Still no answer.

He skipped up the steps and peered into each room, finding them all empty. If she wasn't in the house, where could she have gone? He stood in the bedroom, flipping open the laptop. Gratitude. The password seemed so simple, but it also wasn't that common. The laptop pulled up the main screen. He closed it again. No need in looking through everything just yet. Right now, he felt he needed to find Felicity more. He pulled the glove from his hand and shoved it in his pocket with the evidence bag. Then he loped down the steps and straight out the front door. The blue of the sky had darkened overhead, already turning black to the east. A golden glow from the sun was barely visible over the horizon to the west.

JJ stood at the gate still, his front end on the top of the fence while his back feet remained on the ground. Darren frowned. Why hadn't he really noticed before? He'd thought the dog had been left outside while Felicity was in the house, but now he realized that the golden retriever had given him the clue all along that Felicity was on the other side of the gate, for certain. Darren walked up to the dog and could see the distress in JJ's face. He patted the dog on the head and pushed him down and away from the gate again. Then he opened it, but before he could command the dog to stay, JJ dashed out through the gap.

Darren frowned.

"Hey! That dog can't be running around like that." Perfect timing for the groundskeeper, Mr. Page, to drive up in his ATV. He pulled to a stop and jumped out. His face was distraught, his hands fisted. His posture looked as though he was ready for a fight. "Where is that woman? I've told her a dozen times already to keep this dog on a leash. Liz wouldn't approve of this. Not one bit."

"I'm looking for Felicity now. She wouldn't just leave JJ like this. Have you seen her?" Darren tried to deflect, but the man still kept his eyes on the golden who sniffed at the bottom of the door to the wine store.

Mr. Page grabbed a bit of rope from the back of his ATV. "Not for hours. She was talking to Mr. Anderson."

Then JJ began scratching a bit at the door.

"Hey! Stop that, you stinking mutt. I can't be having to refinish the floor because you scratched it all up."

The golden stopped, sat, and looked up at Darren with a whine.

Darren frowned. "Is she in the wine store?"

Mr. Page shook his head. "Everyone's gone for the day. It's all locked up. There's no way she'd still be in there." He stepped up to the dog and looped the twine he had through the dog collar and tied a quick knot. Then he set the other end in Darren's hand. "When you find that woman, could you please make sure she keeps her dog restrained?"

The coarse, thin rope lay across his palm, and Darren fisted his hand around it. He pulled out his phone and hit redial. Maybe Felicity would answer this time. Then he heard the echo of the ring in the distance. He pulled the phone away from his face. There it was again. The ringtone sounded distant, but it was coming from inside the building.

The older man had started back toward his groundskeeping SUV.

"Wait. Come here. Do you hear that?"

Mr. Page grumbled but started back toward Darren begrudgingly. The ringing stopped. "I don't hear nothing."

"Hold on a second." Darren punched the buttons on his phone to hang up and redial. Then the ringing began again in the distance. Gooseflesh rose on his arms. The first time, he thought it might be Felicity's phone, but now he was certain of it. "I'm going to have to ask you to unlock this door."

Frown lines deepened on the groundskeeper's face. "Is that a phone ringing?"

"It's Felicity's phone. I've dialed it twice and it's ringing from inside. I'm going to need to take a look around. Could you please unlock this door?" Something didn't seem right about this situation, and Darren found his free hand resting on the butt of his gun. Why would Felicity be inside the wine store when everyone had gone for the night?

"Fine. But the dog stays out here. Health code."

Mr. Page began flipping through the large set of keys he'd had stuffed in his pocket, searching for the right one to the doorway.

Darren tied the dog to one of the posts on the front porch with the twine, peering through the windows, but finding nothing but darkness inside, barely lit blue by a soda machine near the back of the store.

When the groundskeeper finally opened the door, Darren drew his gun.

"Is that really necessary?" Mr. Page sucked in a breath.

He peered down at the man and said, "Hopefully not," and then he stepped inside.

Darkness shrouded the room, and Darren lead with his gun arm aimed in front of him. If Felicity was inside with the murderer, he wanted to be prepared. His molars ached from his biting down hard on them, and his ears rang. Anger and dread welled up at the thought that something might have happened to her. If she was hurt in any way, he'd never forgive himself for running late.

With his thumb, he dialed the phone again. The lights overhead flicked on as Mr. Page came in behind him. "Is there anything I can do?" he asked.

"Stay back but keep your eyes open."

The phone started ringing. Because they were close, the ringtone sounded louder. The noise led them to toward the back of the bar and building. He leaned against the metal door leading to the kitchen and peered in. The lights were off inside, but he could see the flash of the screen on the countertop within. After taking a deep breath, he slipped inside, brandishing his weapon in both directions to make sure there was no one hiding in the dark within. He stepped in and toward the phone, lowering his gun once he was sure that no one was there.

Mr. Page came in behind him and flicked on the light overhead.

Darren squinted and blinked at the sudden brightness. He frowned.

"Looks like it was just her phone in here. I wonder what she was doing in the kitchen in the first place." Mr. Page peeked at the countertop. "Someone sliced some of the bread leftover for the staff."

Darren looked at the countertop and saw that things looked unfinished and uneaten. Felicity could have been getting ready to do something with the sliced bread, and then the perpetrator interrupted her. Had she been taken? His stomach flipped in response to his train of thought. He didn't like where they were taking him, but he couldn't understand where she would have gone if she wasn't in the kitchen with her phone. Why was she here when there was food in plenty at Liz's house? Would she have been comfortable here alone? Who was with her, and what happened to her now?

Too many questions flooded his mind.

"Well, I don't see that girl anywhere in here unless she's hiding under the table." The old man put his hands on his hips and his face pulled into a scowl. "You were getting all riled up as if there was a burglar in here or something."

Darren shook his head and re-holstered his weapon. His response had been a bit extreme. Still, he wasn't ready to give up this search. "What else is in here? Is there a cellar?"

"Yeah, but we have to go out and to the side of the building to access it."

"That's fine. Take me there. I just want to look everywhere we can here before I call this in. As of right now, Miss Stilton is missing."

The old man lifted an eyebrow. "I thought that

the police didn't consider a person missing until 24-hours had passed."

A frown tugged at Darren's lip. "This is a murder investigation and Miss Stilton is a witness."

The tired, half-lidded look to the groundskeeper's eyes disappeared as they widened. "Murder? Who? What?"

Darren clenched his teeth again. He hadn't quite been ready to let that one out of the bag, especially not to a potential suspect. Now this man would be on his guard when questioned about the situation, but right now he had to throw the idea of keeping things under wraps out the window. He needed to find Felicity, and he needed this man to be willing to help. Now.

Mr. Page pushed the swinging door to the kitchen back open and led Darren across the hardwood floor, past the bar, and back to the front door. But the moment he opened it, a yellow blur pushed its way in and darted past them both. The thin rope that had tied JJ to the post outside seemed shorter and frayed as he ran past. The twine had broken.

"That dog can't be in here!" the old man hissed.

But Darren smiled. This was it. JJ had been telling him the whole time that he knew where

Felicity was, and the determination in the dog's gait only proved that the dog still knew. It was time for Darren to start listening to him. He darted after the dog, ignoring the old man's shouting and cursing.

JJ stood and pushed on the swinging door, making his way into the kitchen area. Darren came in close behind him. When JJ darted around the counter where Felicity's phone was, his nose sniffed along the ground. Was he finding her scent? Would the dog really know where she is now, or just where she was?

After a moment of circling around the area of the kitchen where Darren already knew Felicity had been, the dog darted to the left and straight toward the large metal door to the walk-in cooler near the corner of the kitchen.

"Unsanitary," the old man grumbled from behind Darren as he walked into the kitchen.

"What's in there?" He pointed to the metal door.

"It's the refrigerator."

"Does it lock from the outside?"

"No, but opening it from the inside is a bit tricky; you have to know how to pull the door handle just right and upward."

Darren rushed over to the doorway and yanked the refrigerator door open. The moment the door pulled free, whatever had been standing against the door fell toward him. He caught her freezing cold form. Felicity.

Shivers racked her whole body, and her teeth chattered as she looked up at him with her warm blue eyes. "D... D... Darren."

The tightening in his chest intensified. He pulled her to his chest and lowered them both slightly toward the ground. Shooting a glance toward the groundskeeper, he said, "Call 9-1-1. We need an ambulance."

"N... no. I'll be fine. I just need to warm up..p..p." Her voice was hoarse.

He frowned down at her. "Let the ambulance come. If you're doing better by the time the paramedics get here, fine. But if not, you're going to the hospital."

She nodded but couldn't control the movement well.

Mr. Page talked quietly on the phone several feet away. Which was a relief to Darren that someone was here to help him. He didn't want to let her go. Her arms and torso were so very cold to the touch, and her lips weren't quite blue yet, but they were pale. He could feel her pulling the heat off his body, and he was just fine with that.

JJ laid his body right next to Felicity's legs, lending her his warmth as well. Their bond was something Darren had never seen before. He knew that golden retrievers were loyal and loving dogs, but he had no idea how useful JJ would be in both helping him find Felicity and helping now to get her body temperature up.

"Here, take this." Mr. Page handed them a jacket which Darren immediately wrapped around Felicity. "I'm going to warm up some water for hot cocoa."

He nodded up at the old man. The sour expression the man had earlier had fled. Darren had respect for that. He'd much rather have a person with a cool head around to help with a dire situation than someone he had to tell what to do because of panic or surliness.

A few moments later, as her shivers were calming a little, the man brought over a warm cup. "I didn't want to make it too hot, so it's just a little warmer than tepid. I'm going to head outside to wait for the ambulance and guide them in. Will you two be okay?"

Darren nodded.

With a firm nod, the man ducked out the swinging kitchen door. Jay lifted his head to watch the man go and then rested his chin on Felicity's thigh. Darren pressed the cup toward her lips. Her eyes were closed.

"Drink some of this; it will help."

When she opened her eyes, the shivers came back a little bit harder. As if going into a more sleep-like state had helped her gain some control over her body's autonomic response, but now that she was fully awake again, she couldn't help herself. She took a slow sip of the liquid, her eyes going half-lidded again. "I'm s… sorry," she said.

Darren frowned. "What? You've got nothing to be sorry about."

"I l… locked myself in the f… f… fridge."

"It's fine. Don't worry about it."

"Mr. Page c… came into the k… kitchen, but he couldn't hear me yelling that I w… was inside the cooler. H… he shut off the l… lights and left. Mr. Anderson l… looked in the window, but because the l… lights were off, he left, too."

His frown deepened. "You saw Mr. Anderson, too?"

She nodded and took the cup he was holding and held it in her hands. "It feels good to hold it," she said as she took a sip. When she pulled her hands away, she looked into Darren's eyes. "He was helping me make a s... sandwich. He got called away. I w... went into the cooler to get stuff, but got l... locked in. He came back about a half-hour l... later, but the lights were off, and he couldn't s... see me."

She took another sip of the warm liquid. Her body started to settle down, and she was shaking less. Her limbs still felt unbearably cold to the touch. "How long were you in there for?" he asked.

After shaking her head, she said, "S... soon after I got off the phone with you."

His jaw clenched. She'd been in there for more than two hours. That was way too long to be exposed in temperatures close to freezing in nothing more than shorts and a knit crew shirt.

"They're here," Mr. Page said as he opened the door and the paramedics entered the kitchen.

ALMOST AN HOUR LATER, Felicity was on her feet, waving goodbye to the paramedics as they started down the long driveway away from the winery. They'd checked her vitals and told her to stay as warm as possible for the rest of the night, and to head to the emergency room if she felt numbness in her extremities or any issues with fatigue or dizziness. She wrapped the oversized canvas jacket around herself. It smelled of tobacco and unfamiliar musky male, but she was just thankful to have its warmth.

Jay sat on her feet. It was as if he knew she'd just been in danger of being hurt and wanted to stay as close as possible to her. Darren stood next to her, an arm around her shoulders the whole time as they stood. But when they'd been sitting on the floor earlier, she'd been in his lap.

Heat rose to her face as she thought about it for the first time. How embarrassing. But also, how comforting. He'd been a source of warmth and safety, like she couldn't ever remember feeling before.

"Keep the jacket for now. You can return it later." Mr. Page scowled and then turned his back to her as he headed toward the older model truck sitting at the far end of the lot.

"Thank you," she called to his retreating form, but he didn't respond with anything more than a wave of his hand.

They stood and watched the man's truck start

its way down the long driveway. For a moment, Felicity didn't speak, she just savored the sounds of the crickets singing in the night air and the warmth of the wind blowing through. Panic had gripped her when she was stuck in the restaurant cooler. She thought that she'd be stuck there through the night at least. Because of the fact that so much of her skin was exposed, she worried she wouldn't make it. Then the tears had come, wetting the skin of her face and neck, making the cold air that blew on her that much worse.

Her heart squeezed in her chest. She didn't know if she'd make it. All because she was stupid and let the fridge door close behind her. She wrapped her arms around herself.

Darren squeezed her shoulder slightly. "Do you want me to drive you home, or follow you?"

She frowned, realizing the urgency of the time. "Did you lose the case already?"

His free hand went to the back of his neck, where it rubbed as he smiled sheepishly. "No, I haven't. My lieutenant wants me to wrap it up, but he's given me a little bit of time. I'm not sure if we can find anything substantial up at the house, but my gut is telling me there's something more going on here."

Her shoulders dropped a little in relief. She shrugged out of his hold gently and took a step forward. Jay leapt to his feet to follow. "Then if you're up for it, let's go up to the house and I'll show you what I found on Liz's laptop."

Darren's brow went up. "If I'm up for it? What about you?"

"I can handle it." She nodded.

He shook his head. "You barely let the paramedics look at you and now you're saying your fine to keep working this case? It makes me wonder if you truly know your limits."

She shrugged. "I guess I don't since I've never reached them."

His eyes sparkled in the moonlight as he laughed. "Well, let's not push them now, okay."

She laughed with him. "Deal."

A stomach growl broke the quiet of the night. Felicity's arms wrapped around her torso for a moment, but then she realized it hadn't been her stomach. She peered up at Darren whose hand was rubbing the back of his neck again. "Sorry about that. I really need to get something to eat, too. You up for dinner?"

Jay had sat next to her and leaned against her leg again. "I don't think I can leave JJ right now.

He's being a little clingy because of everything that happened this afternoon."

"Then let's call in for pizza. I'm sure they deliver out here."

A wide smile spread across her face. "Sounds like a plan."

Chapter Nine

FELICITY WOKE when the sun slashed bright light across her face from an east facing window. She blinked at it and covered her eyes. Stiffness seized her neck the moment she tried to move. Why did she wake up sitting upright on couch in an unfamiliar living room? She blinked about some more. A pizza box sat on the table in front of her and a quilt had been draped over her body. On the other end of the couch, Darren Willis slept in an upright position similar to hers.

Her heart fluttered at the sight of him. Over the years his face had become hardened, manlier and more angled than it had been back in high school, but with his eyes closed, asleep in the morning light, the boyish, angelic look returned with the softness of his expression.

The night before they had gone through Liz's financial records while waiting for the pizza to arrive. Once it came they'd settled in and put on the television playing low in the background while they talked. And talked. They'd shared what they'd done with their lives since they'd last seen each other in high school while feeding their crusts to Jay, since she hadn't brought him any dog food. Late into the night, they just talked with each other like old friends catching up. Then somewhere along the way, she'd fallen asleep… and so had he. Who had fallen asleep first? She wasn't sure. But she didn't remember having the quilt on her the way she did now.

A musical beat played on the television, signifying the start of Good Morning Gold Coast, the local talk show that started at seven a.m. Felicity stretched her neck to the left and then to the right to get the kink out of it. And then sat up further, letting the quilt fall from her shoulders to her lap. Jay stood from his sleeping position on the floor by her feet and set his head on her lap. "Good morning, sunshine," she said as she scratched his ears and leaned down to give him a hug.

She grabbed her phone from the coffee table and shot a text message to the vice principal that she'd need another day off from work today due to her birthmother's death. It was likely time to visit with the lawyer about the estate, so that she could wrap up that situation as well. Once the text was sent, she stood slowly, trying not to disturb Darren just yet, and placed the quilt that had been on her body gently over Darren's lap. He shifted just a bit, and for a moment, Felicity had thought she'd woken him, but his eyes remained closed and his face relaxed.

On tiptoes, she headed into the kitchen to start a pot of coffee. But once she got there, she realized that Liz didn't drink coffee by the pot. Instead, she had one of those single-serve coffee pod machines. It took Felicity about fifteen minutes to figure it out, but soon she had two steaming cups of coffee sitting on the countertop, smelling delicious.

"Hey, good morning," Darren's deep baritone said from behind her, still slightly groggy with sleep.

Felicity didn't know if she'd ever heard anything in her life that was more appealing. She turned toward him with a cup in each hand and a wide smile. "How do you take your coffee?"

A grin spread across his face. "Cream and sugar. Do you have it?"

She gestured with a nod toward the lazy Susan on the counter. He laughed, took a cup from her hands, and set it back on the counter to add the things he needed to make his perfect cup.

After taking a long draft of her own mug, she opened the fridge, finding eggs and cheese. "I've got what I need here to whip us up a couple of quick omelets if you're game."

He checked the time on his phone. "I don't know that I have time. I've got to leave in twenty."

"It's fine! I'll make omelet sandwiches on toast; you can eat and run."

"Really," he said, lifting a brow. "That would be great."

Although there was a slight learning curve that she had to make in order to figure out all of Liz's appliances, Felicity still managed to put together two sandwiches, toasted on the same homemade bread from the wine store's bar and restaurant. When she took a bite, she found the bread was some of the best she'd eaten.

Darren wrapped his sandwich in a paper towel and downed the last bit of his second cup of coffee.

He moaned after taking a bite. "This is great. Thank you."

"No problem," she said around a mouthful of her own.

"Sorry that I need to get going so early."

"No problem. I understand that it's only Thursday. Not everyone has the day off."

He nodded. "You took leave from work then?"

"Yesterday and today. I have to make arrangements with the funeral home and talk to the lawyer about settling this estate."

"I'm sorry we couldn't find enough evidence to keep the case open. I guess we'll have to consider the possibility that this was a suicide after all. There's nothing specific enough to suggest otherwise except our hunches."

She nodded. "I understand that… and I'm starting to accept it."

He stood and started toward the door, taking another bite of his food. "That's good… and so is this sandwich."

"Thank you for coming last night. I had a really good time. I guess this is it since the case is closed." She frowned, trying to hint at the fact that she wanted to see him again, but her gaze dropped toward his shoes, as she was afraid to meet his eyes and see the rejection that might be there.

He cleared his throat. "Actually, I'd like to see you again, if you think you might have the time."

Her gaze shot up and she lifted a brow. "Are you asking me out, detective, because without an actual date and time, one might think you were generalizing enough to brush me off later."

The Adam's apple on his neck bobbed as he swallowed, his eyes growing wide. "Not at all—I mean, how about Saturday? Are you busy?"

A smile spread across her face making her cheeks hurt. "Nope. Not busy."

His empty hand shot to the back of his neck, and he began rubbing it again. Now she was recognizing it as a habit he had whenever he was shy or embarrassed. How sweet. Was she actually making him a bit shy? Darren Willis?

"Great. Then I'll give you a call so we can set up something. It's my day off."

She nodded. "Sounds good."

And with that bit of awkwardness, he stepped out the screen door and onto the porch. She watched him as he virtually skipped down the walkway to his sedan, finishing the sandwich before he'd even made it to the gate and then shoving the paper towel into the pocket of his jeans.

Darren Willis had just asked her out. It would have been her high school dream come true. Who was she kidding? It was still her dream come true. The Darren she'd known in school was handsome, popular, but always kind enough to open doors for people and even help them when they were in trouble. He didn't seem to remember it, but there was a time when they were in a business class together and two boys were picking on her. He'd stood up for her and got them both to quit by asking if they'd like him to start treating them the same way. They didn't mess with her again. But he'd done it so flippantly that it likely didn't even make an impression on him. It had made one on her, though. It was the reason she'd started the crush on him in the first place. Darren wasn't just handsome even back then. He was also kind and protective, just when she'd needed him.

And she still needed that in her life.

Her phone vibrated on the coffee table, drawing her attention back to the present. She stepped over to the phone, giving Jay the last bit of her sandwich. "Sorry, boy. We'll get home and get you fed in a short bit."

She picked up the phone and found text messages from both the vice principal and Georgia. Her heart sank. She hadn't told Georgia anything about what had happened the night before, and worse, she didn't want to see what the response was going to be from Mr. Jordan. Her fingers scrolled to see Georgia's message first.

Hey Girl. Where you at?

She typed a quick response. *Will be home shortly. At Liz's.*

OK take your time, but let your Wifey know when you're going to spend the night elsewhere, OK?

Sorry. Will pick up donuts on the way home. :)

Promises. Promises.

Felicity still had a smile on her face as she steeled herself and opened Mr. Jordan's text message.

We understand and are sad to hear that your birth-mother has passed, but if we are doing well without your presence over the next few days, the board will have to discuss the necessity of your position in the first place. Please be aware and give notice sooner if you need more time.

The smile slid from her face. He was right. The notice she'd given yesterday at four-thirty in the morning was unfair. And today it had been seven. She was already on his bad side; she shouldn't go pushing his buttons. She took a deep breath and then texted back.

I'm sorry about the short notice. I find out when the funeral is today and will let you know as soon as possible if I need tomorrow as well. Thank you for understanding. As she hit send, she thanked God for text messages. At least didn't need to talk to the man on the phone or in person.

After sticking her phone in the back pocket of her jeans shorts, she picked up Liz's quilt from the couch and folded it, placing it on the back of the sofa once more. She stepped into the kitchen and did the dishes really quickly as well. Then she took a last look around before heading outside in the morning sunlight. The light breeze made her wish for a sweater as goosebumps rose on her arms. And for a brief moment, she remembered the feeling of the cold air in the fridge blowing on her when she'd been locked in the night before. A shiver ran through her at the thought. That was an experience she'd never like to repeat.

As she reached the gate, she noticed two cars in the lot; Mr. Page and Mr. Anderson were both already at the winery. She peered around and found that the groundskeeping ATV had already gone, meaning the Mr. Page had left with it. She breathed a sigh of relief as she opened the gate and gave Jay the command, "Stay by."

Like the perfectly trained therapy dog he was, Jay stayed immediately next to her thigh as she turned around and latched the gate behind her.

"I'm so glad to hear you're okay." Heath's excited voice reached her as the door to the wine store slammed shut behind him. He hopped down from the porch and strode toward her in four long strides. The newspaper he'd been holding dropped to the ground and his hands landed on her shoulders—his brow wrinkled with worry. "I had no idea you were still in the cooler when I'd left. I thought you'd ducked out after eating your sandwiches, like I'd told you to. You could have been hurt."

She offered him a sheepish smile. "I'm fine. No harm done. Forget about it."

"I'm so sorry. It's all my fault."

"No way. It's not your fault. It's mine. Please, don't trouble yourself over it."

He let out a slow breath, his gaze darting from one of her eyes to the other. "You're sure you're okay?"

She nodded. "I'm sure."

His hands released her shoulders and relief

smoothed the lines on his face. "Have you eaten breakfast yet? Join me at the bar. My treat."

She smiled and shook her head. "Thank you for the offer, but I've really got to go. Jay hasn't eaten breakfast yet, and I promised my roommate that I'd bring home donuts."

He laughed but nodded. "Okay then. Drive safely."

"Thank you," she said, looking around. "Do you always come in so early? I thought the tours didn't start until ten."

One of his eyebrows quirked. "I like getting an early start. It keeps the workers, like Mr. Page, on their toes."

"Really? He seems like a diligent worker."

"It's the reason *why* he's so diligent." He laughed. "Even now, he's back out in the fields looking for snakes so they don't interfere with the tours. Apparently, he's an ophiophilist."

She blinked. "A what?"

"Oh?" he asked with a chuckle. "You don't know what that means either, huh? Mr. Page just informed me—it means snake lover. He insists on catching the things live and relocating them."

"Wow." Felicity could hardly imagine. "So, the old man does have a heart."

Heath lifted a brow and gave her a half-smile. "You couldn't tell by looking at him, huh?"

She laughed and shook her head, feeling a little guilty at poking fun at the old man again.

"Well, have a good day. Talk to you later," Heath said with a wave as he started back to the wine store.

She nodded to him, and then noticed the newspaper he'd dropped earlier still on the ground. There were hand-written notes and circles in red ink on the page, and at first, she thought it was a crossword puzzle. "You forgot your paper," she called out as she picked it up.

Then she noticed that the page was in the sports section and times were circled as well as notes scribbled in the margin, but she only recognized the words, win, place, and show before the paper was snatched from her hand.

Heath's smile remained frozen on his face as he tucked the paper under his arm. "Thanks so much; I hadn't finished reading the sports section."

She shrugged and smiled. "No problem. My father is an avid paper reader as well."

He clutched his chest and feigned pain there. "No… please tell me you didn't just compare me to your father. Hopefully I'm not *that* old."

She laughed. "No way. You're much younger. No worries there."

"Phew." He sighed with relief and then waved his paper toward her as he started back onto the porch of the wine store.

She laughed and pulled the handle on the hatch of her SUV to let Jay hop into the back of the vehicle. Once inside, he turned about and waited for her to pat him on the head—which she did before closing the hatch and making sure he was secure. With a long sigh, she looked around at the quiet morning once more. Heath had been right. The winery would be a great location for a bed and breakfast. It was quiet enough out here to feel like a bit of country even though the main city of Redwood Cove wasn't far away at all.

She smiled and got into the driver's seat of her car, starting the engine and rolling her neck again to get that kink out before backing the SUV up. Soft music played low on the radio as her phone connected wirelessly and started the last playlist she'd been listening to on her last drive. She pulled down the narrow drive, having to pull over and stop once to allow another car to come in with a purple shirted employee to pass her. They waved, and she returned the gesture.

In her mind, she mapped out her route to the donut shop as she pulled out onto the main street and accelerated to the speed limit for the area, which was forty-five. She'd be back in town and at Cup of Joe's diner in less than fifteen minutes and would pick up some of those cream-filled chocolate donuts that Georgia liked so much.

The sun shone through the back of the car, glinting off her rearview mirror, into her eyes. She leaned forward to push the rearview mirror into a better position when she heard it. The scratching rattle of a snake and a hissing noise. Then something slithered across her left leg.

Chapter Ten

FELICITY'S HEART raced in her chest and everything felt as though it were going in slow motion. She jerked the wheel to the right and slammed on the brakes at the same time. The sudden change in speed and trajectory sent her car spinning. The SUV tilted into a ditch and landed somewhat on the passenger side. The snake was thrown to that side of the vehicle as well. The brown pattern across its body coiled as it looked up at her. She met eyes with it as she clung to her seatbelt.

Had it bitten her? She racked her brain but didn't remember feeling any pain. She eyed the back kennel where Jay looked at her through the rearview mirror. He was panting. What if the snake had bitten him? *Oh God, please let him be all right.*

"Are you okay?" an older gentleman came to the door of her car and peered in. His voice was muffled by the closed window. "I saw the whole thing. I already called the police. What happened?"

Felicity pointed to the rattlesnake that still lay coiled on the passenger door. "Can you help me?"

"Good Lord!" The man's eyes grew wide as his hand ran through his graying hair. He nodded and helped her pull the door open. "Take my hand. Hold onto me while I undo your seatbelt."

"Thank you so much." Felicity clung to him while he pulled the seatbelt free and helped lift her from the vehicle. All the while she attempted to keep her feet away from where the snake sat in her car.

Once her feet were solid ground, she looked down at her vehicle in the culvert. How on Earth had the snake gotten in there? The only person she knew who had been handling the snakes was Mr. Curtis Page. Could he be trying to kill her? Was he the one who killed Liz? She rushed to the back of the SUV and pulled open the hatch. "JJ! Are you okay?"

The golden retriever wagged his tail and hopped down as soon as the hatch was opened. Tears filled Felicity's eyes as she leaned down and searched Jay's legs and body for any blood or sign of a bite.

Sirens wailed in the distance.

The gentleman who'd helped her from the car put a hand on her shoulder. "Are you sure you're okay? Were you bitten by that thing? Step back and I'll close the hatch. Let's try to keep the snake inside for the moment."

She nodded and stepped back. A police car pulled up behind her SUV, and it was followed by an unmarked sedan with a blue siren on the dashboard. Darren hopped out of the car, and relief flooded her. Her knees felt weak, and the tears she'd been holding back broke free and spilled over her cheeks. A sob pulled its way up her throat.

When he reached her, he pulled her into his arms and just held her tightly while she sobbed in the darkness as his chest blocked out all sun.

DARREN THOUGHT he'd have a heart attack when he heard the description of the vehicle involved in an accident on the highway from the winery. When they said the license plate—READWJJ—he whipped around and rushed back to the scene. Now he held her in his arms while she fell to pieces. The strong, stalwart Felicity who sent away the paramedic yesterday was nowhere to be found.

The gentleman who called in the incident, Mr. Stokes, told him the story as best as he could with the information he understood. The uniformed police officer called for a tow truck and for animal control to handle the snake. Jay sat right next to Felicity the whole while, not letting his eyes off of her. The depths of the dog's loyalty knew no bounds.

Once Mr. Stokes had finished his relaying of what happened, Felicity seemed calmer and pushed herself away from Darren just enough to look up into his face. "It's Mr. Page. I think he's trying to kill me. He's the one who shut off the light when I was in the cooler, and he's been catching and releasing the rattlesnakes at the winery."

Darren frowned. He didn't want to argue with her, but she was on the verge of hysterics. And though Mr. Page had been surly, he'd helped Darren when they found Felicity trapped in the cooler. Was the old man really capable of murder? "Let's not jump to conclusions, Felicity. Are you hurt?"

She frowned up at him, the wrinkles in her forehead deepening. "But I know it's true. He's a bad man. Liz probably fired him, and he killed her in retaliation. Now he's trying to kill me because… because…"

Pulling her closer, Darren squeezed her in his arms. "It's okay. Just stay calm. It is possible if there were snakes on the property that one could make it into your car all on its own because it sat in the same place all day yesterday and overnight. Now, are you hurt?"

A sigh escaped her. "I'm not hurt."

"Maybe we should get you to Gold Coast Regional Hospital, anyway, and checked out. We don't know if—"

"Really, I'm fine. I don't want to go to the hospital."

He frowned, not getting why she was always so resistant to taking care of herself.

"I need to keep an eye on JJ though. If he was bitten by the snake, I don't know what I'll do." She hugged the golden closer to her leg.

"Let's get you and JJ home, then." Darren started guiding her back to his sedan. "Animal control will take care of the snake, and then the tow truck will take your SUV to the shop. They'll call me and let me know which one. We can pick it up later once they've given it a once-over, okay?"

She nodded, her gaze still cast toward the ground.

Silence settled between them on the drive back to her house, but it was a comfortable silence, with soft music from his radio playing in the background and the occasional static and talk over his police band. Felicity seemed deep in thought, and JJ just lay comfortably on the backseat of his sedan. When they drew near town, she perked up. "Could we stop by the diner there and get some donuts?"

He nodded and pulled into the small lot, even though the request seemed a little odd.

Once the car came to a complete stop, Felicity undid her safety belt. "I'll just pop in and grab a half dozen. I'll be right back."

Even though he lifted an eyebrow at her behavior, he was glad to see Felicity acting somewhat normal after the stressful ordeal she'd gone through yesterday and the accident today. One thing was certain—it did seem like too much of a coincidence that she'd locked herself in the restaurant cooler yesterday on her own, and then a rattlesnake just happened to make its way into her car... all on its own.

She ducked into the diner, and he watched her through the glass windows as she smiled at the man behind the counter. After a short conversation while the man loaded a box for her, she paid and was soon right back out, heading toward the car, a soft smile still gracing her face.

Jay stood in the backseat as she approached the car and opened the door. "My roommate Georgia loves the donuts here, but we rarely get out this way to pick them up because it's on the opposite end of town from us. Since we were out this way for the winery, I promised to pick up a box."

She lifted the lid on the box and pointed it out toward Darren.

"Want one?"

He smiled back at her. The rebound from the incident with the snake had happened faster than expected. Felicity seemed like the type to not let her emotions rule her for very long. She was sensible. He liked that about her. He peered into the box. "Is that blueberry?"

"Yes! Those are my favorite—blueberry donuts coated in glaze. The others are chocolate covered with a light cream in the middle—Georgia's favorite."

"Well you only got six of them. I don't want to take one away from either of you."

She shook her head and half-laughed. Her nose crinkled in an incredibly cute way. "The last thing either of us need is three donuts all to ourselves. Feel free to take one of each if you like."

"I'll take one of the blueberry. I haven't had a good blueberry donut in a long time."

"You haven't had the donuts here?"

"I have, but not the blueberry." He grabbed one between his finger and thumb and guided it straight for his lips. The crispy glaze on the outside gave the donut the only structure. The inside was the softest, melt in your mouth, blueberry flavored heaven he'd ever tasted. "This is awesome."

"I know, right?" She smiled even wider as she closed the box and set her donut on the top of it while she buckled her seat belt.

After sharing their donuts with each other, the silence had been broken, and Felicity was back to filling the drive with anecdotes and stories about life with the kids she worked with, the golden retriever in the backseat, and even her roommate. Darren loved listening to the soft lilt of her voice. It made him feel at ease in a way that he'd never experienced with anyone that he could remember, except for his mother. And he could barely remember those kinds of things about her since she had died when he was so young.

They pulled into the driveway of the ranch home but stayed in the car for two minutes longer while she finished telling the last story about how JJ had had nearly jumped into the shower with her the first time she tried to take one without him in the bathroom. Then she suddenly blushed. "I guess really, talking about bathroom behavior is a bit too much information."

He laughed. "It's fine. I like that you feel open with me."

After a sigh, she asked, "Would you like to come in for coffee? Maybe another donut?"

"I wish I could, but I really need to check in at the station." Dread filled his heart upon those words. It was time to close the case, but it made Darren feel like he was closing the door on the closeness he'd achieved with Felicity at the same time. Sure, he'd asked her out and she'd accepted, but would it feel forced once they started trying to date? Their growing affection for each other had felt so natural as they'd spent more time with each other on this case.

She bit her bottom lip, then nodded and

unbuckled her seatbelt. Silently she started out of the car, closed her door, and opened the one in the back to let out the golden retriever. Before closing that door, she ducked her head in again. "Will you check with the towing company about my SUV and give me a call or text me?"

"Of course." His heart fluttered a bit in his chest at the thought of getting to talk to her again today.

Her face brightened a bit in response. "Great. Then I'll talk to you later."

He nodded, and she shut the door. There was a lilt in her step as she walked, balancing the box of donuts in one hand as JJ jumped around her in an excited circle. It seemed that even the dog was happy to be home finally after the hardships the two of them had shared the last few days.

After she'd made it into the house, Darren pulled the car in reverse and headed to the police station. The lieutenant sat against Darren's desk as he walked into the building.

"Glad to see you finally made it in." The lieutenant frowned. "It's already well after nine."

Darren frowned in return. "I was near the call of an accident this morning, so I helped the uniformed officer and the driver in the situation."

The lines in the lieutenant's forehead deepened. "Were there any casualties?"

"No, sir."

He nodded. "You do know that responding to accidents is no longer your job. You have cases on your desk that need settling. Witnesses to question. You cannot let irrelevant things distract you from your duties."

"Yes, sir."

"Close the suicide case at the winery today. Start on the case at the Highland hotel. There's been a rash of robberies there, and one of the staff is suspect."

"Yes, sir."

The lieutenant lifted an eyebrow and looked Darren up and down before pushing off the edge of the desk and starting toward his office.

A sigh escaped Darren's lips. The closer he came to closing the case on the winery, the more it seemed that the feeling there was foul play involved became more likely. He grabbed the stack of folders on his desk and decided to get the questioning done at the hotel, and since the hotel wasn't too far from the winery, he'd stop in and ask a few questions about the snakes there as well.

Chapter Eleven

FELICITY HUNG up the phone with the funeral home and blew out a long breath. Sunlight poured into the kitchen from the window above the sink, but there was still the slightest chill in the air. She gripped her coffee mug with two hands, letting the warmth seep into her skin. Did she still feel this way from being in the cooler the night before? She just couldn't seem to get warm enough.

Georgia sat across the table from her with a worried expression and a lifted eyebrow. "Are you okay?"

"The funeral's tomorrow morning." She pursed her lips and then took a sip from her mug.

"I'm really sorry, honey. I'll take off work tomorrow to come and support you."

A weight lifted from Felicity's shoulders at the sound of her friend's words. "Thank you."

Georgia winked. "What are friends for?"

Speaking of taking off from work... Felicity picked up her phone and shot off another text message to the vice principal. At least he wouldn't complain about short notice this time. He quickly sent one back.

Sorry for your loss. Will you be back to work on Monday, then?

At least the funeral was on a Friday, so she could spend the rest of the weekend off and working with the lawyer to settle the estate. It definitely wasn't unreasonable to think that she and Jay could be back to work on Monday. She texted him back that she planned to be back to work on Monday. And she truly hoped that would be the end of the talk of her position being eliminated.

But she knew it wouldn't be.

For some reason the vice principal believed her job was frivolous and unnecessary. There might be others on the board of the school who felt the same. No matter. Once she started showing results for her hard work, those thoughts would be quashed. All she needed to do was get the results started. She thought about little Addison, and how the child likely missed her time with Jay already. Yes, she'd definitely be back to work on Monday.

Her phone rang—this time it was from an unknown number. She hesitated a moment, meeting eyes with her roommate who just shrugged and took another bite of her cream donut. Not much help there. She hit the green button to accept the call and then answered, "Hello?"

"Hi, Ms. Stilton, this is Lucian Wright, Elizabeth Collier's lawyer. The estate is settling a few of Ms. Collier's personal debts—which were few, by the way—but I need you to come sign a few checks for me as executor so that I release the money."

"Oh! Okay. Do you need me to come by your office?"

"Actually, I'm at the winery right now. Can you come by here?"

Dread poured down her back like cold water. Her mouth became dry. Although she tried to tell herself that Darren was right, and the snake had gotten into her car of its own accord, she couldn't help but feel that it was sabotage instead—and Mr. Page was definitely the culprit. And even though she knew the incident with the restaurant cooler was accidental, she couldn't get past the fact that it had happened at that place.

Was it all bad luck or just accidental? Either way, she had already begun hating the winery and everything it stood for. If she had her own way, she doubted she'd ever go there again.

"Miss Stilton?"

"Oh." She blinked in surprise, tried to swallow but found it incredibly hard. "I'm sorry, but could we meet at your office instead? I'm not too sure I can get all the way out to the winery right now, as my car is at the repair shop."

"Girl! I got you. You can borrow my car," Georgia said from across the table, unfortunately, loud enough for Mr. Wright to hear as well. The smile across Georgia's face as she slid the keys across the table made the pit of Felicity's stomach flip. What was she supposed to do now?

"So, it seems you're covered then? You have a car?" Mr. Wright pressed. "I have more business to take care of here at the winery, so I'd much prefer if you could meet me here."

Felicity closed her eyes and let out a long breath. She hated fear. She couldn't let it control her, or it always would. Fear was best defeated by facing it head on. She could do this. "Yes, sir. I'll be there shortly."

"Excellent. I'll see you in a short bit then." He

hung up the phone before she could say anything else.

Each of Felicity's joints suddenly felt stiff as she set her phone on the table and looked over at her roommate. Georgia didn't know anything about what had happened to Felicity in the last twenty-four hours, as she'd not had the chance to tell her yet. And now her roommate was on the floor with Jay, loving on him and giving him his breakfast. Lately it seemed that Georgia was doing a better job of taking care of Jay than Felicity had been. She sighed. She hated that Jay had missed his dinner the night before. Pizza crusts did not a meal make, especially not for a hard-working dog like Jay. Felicity looked up at her friend as Georgia drew back up to her feet. "Aren't you working today? Don't you need your car?"

She shook her head. "I already texted Alice. She's coming by to pick me up in twenty."

Felicity frowned. She was stuck doing this, but she'd be smarter this time. Mr. Wright only needed her there to sign a few checks. She'd get the job done out on the covered porch. That way she could keep an eye on Georgia's car and make sure no one messed with it. It wouldn't be hard to make this a quick, direct trip. Get the job done and get out.

Determination coursed through her. She could do this.

DARREN ARRIVED AT THE WINERY, feeling as though he'd only left a short bit ago. One of the purple-shirted employees stood on the covered porch of the wine store, giving a short history of the winery and the sorts of grapes they grew there, as well as the process of making the wine. Darren hopped out of his sedan and watched the talk for just a moment.

As interesting as the topic seemed, Darren had specific questions he needed to ask, and he wanted to find the one person whose name Felicity had called in distress when he'd met her on the side of the road after her accident. Mr. Page stood over his ATV, pouring gas into the tank from a gas can. He called over as he approached. "Morning."

Mr. Page stood up straight, pulling the gas can upright and shading his eyes from the sunlight that was to Darren's back. "What can I do you for, detective?"

"There was an incident this morning that I'd like to ask you a few questions about. I'd heard that the winery has been having a bit of difficulty with rattlesnakes."

The older man frowned, setting the cap back on his gas can and putting it in the bed of the ATV. "I wouldn't call it difficulty. One of the guests on tour complained that she saw one on the trail. I routinely drive the grounds to search for the snakes, capture them, and put them in this box." He patted the top of a plastic box in the back of the ATV. "Then at the end of the day, I drive them about eight miles down the road, past Pacific Adventures, and release them in the park. I have permission from the park rangers to do so."

Darren scrubbed the back of his neck. He was glad that Mr. Page had been willing to divulge so much detail about his process. It had given the detective a moment to process his words, stance, and expressions. "So, you're a snake lover, then?"

"I guess. They have their place in the ecosystem, just like everything else does. We shouldn't end their lives simply because we find them inconvenient to our way of life."

"Fair enough. Do you ever get any issues with the snakes getting into buildings around here, or into cars?"

His frown deepened. "I imagine it's a possibility

either way, but I haven't heard tell of either of those things happening. No."

Darren nodded. Mr. Page seemed surly and hard to get along with, but most men did when they were honest to the point of harshness. "What was your relationship like with Elizabeth Collier?"

The old man's ice blue eyes turned mournful and the wrinkles in his forehead changed as they went from a hard glare to soft sorrow. "She was a friend—a good one. When I came back as a vet from the gulf, I was in a downward spiral. I couldn't find a job, I had no place to go, no family. But Liz gave me a chance to change, a real one and a real hand up. I would have taken a bullet for the woman. I'm sad that I didn't do more for her if she took her own life. And if she didn't, I'm mad that I didn't see what was coming and help."

"I heard that Liz had recently fired her housekeeper and hired a new one. Was there anyone else around whose job was at risk?"

Mr. Page looked confused or half a moment and then lifted an eyebrow. "Not that I heard tell. But Liz didn't discuss her business with me. If anyone knew that kind of thing, I imagine it would be Lucian, the lawyer. Or maybe Heath Anderson."

Darren nodded. "Do you know where I can find Mr. Anderson today?"

Mr. Page glanced at his watch. "It's nearly lunch time, so I imagine he's in the bar. He really likes watching the sports programs on the TV in there."

"Thank you for taking the time to answer my questions, Mr. Page. I know that you're a busy man." Darren backed up two steps to start heading in the direction of the bar and wine store.

"Not a problem. If Liz didn't off herself, you're going to find the guy who did this, right?" He narrowed his gaze at Darren.

Darren stopped his backward retreat for a moment and nodded to the man. "I'll do my best."

The old man jumped into the ATV and sat in his seat. "I guess that's all I can ask for, then." And he started up the engine on the four-wheeler and steered it away toward the rows of vineyard on the other side of the parking lot.

Once Darren had watched him fully leave, he turned around and walked straight to the bar and store area. The employee leading the tour pulled the guests toward the vineyards as she continued her spiel. Once the tour had passed him, Darren stepped onto the covered porch and headed into the wine store. He found Heath sitting at the bar with his half-eaten plate of salad pushed to the side while he wrote notes on the margin of a newspaper and looked up at the horse race playing on the television.

As the race finished, Heath cursed and set his pen on the paper, shoving it to the side and then pulling his salad back over. Darren walked up to him and sat on the stool next to the man. Heath glanced up and lifted a brow in surprise. "Detective?"

"Hello, Mr. Anderson. Enjoying your lunch?"

As if to punctuate his pleasure, he stuffed a forkful of lettuce and chicken into his mouth and then offered a half-smile and a nod.

"Well don't let me stop you, but do you mind if I ask a few questions as you eat?"

Heath's brows knit together. He finished chewing the bite in his mouth, swallowed, and asked, "Is this about Lizzy? I thought it was an open and shut case of suicide?"

Darren shrugged. "Maybe. Maybe not. Where did you say you were the morning in question?"

He pushed the chicken Caesar salad he'd been eating to the side and leaned an elbow on the bar. "Napa. I was staying at a very quiet bed and breakfast there. I'm happy to give you the phone number if you want it."

Darren nodded. "Sure, I'll take it. And how long did you stay at the bed and breakfast?"

Heath looked up toward the ceiling, scratching his chin in thought. "Let's see. I went up there on Saturday and had been there through the weekend for the wine convention. The convention ended Monday night, but I'd gone out with some friends I'd met at the con and decided to stay until Tuesday morning. I got the call from Lucian at about two and immediately came back. You were here when I got back, at whatever time that was… late afternoon."

"Right."

Heath's cellphone, which had been sitting on the bar next to the newspaper, rang. The man's body stiffened, and an unreadable expression twisted his features for a moment as his facial muscles tensed. Slowly, the man turned and glanced at the lit screen on the front of his phone.

Darren peered over as well and saw it was a call from an unknown number.

Without answering, the man turned back to Darren. "Will that be all, detective?"

"You not going to answer that?"

That unreadable expression tensed in his face again. "I don't appreciate spam, so I don't answer if I don't know the number."

Sounded reasonable. Darren shifted gears a little. "Did you know that the walk-in cooler here at the restaurant was tricky to open from the inside?"

His eyes went a little wide. "No. I had no idea. I really don't spend any time in the kitchen here."

"But you allowed Felicity in to make a sandwich?"

"A sandwich is pretty simple, and the restaurant staff leaves the leftover fresh bread out for any of the team members who want to take it home or eat. It's one of the perks that Lizzy had instituted."

Darren nodded. "Do you have any pets?"

Heath lifted a brow. "That's an unusual question. I don't have any dogs or cats. Being around fur too long messes with my allergies. But I've had furless animals like fish in the past."

The man's phone stopped ringing, and his shoulders relaxed. Seemed like odd behavior for just avoiding a spam call. "Well, if you'll give me the name and number of the bed and breakfast where you stayed for the weekend, that'll be all."

After a nod, Heath picked up his phone and pulled up the info on the place where he'd stayed in

Napa. Darren plugged it into his phone, thanked the man, and got up from the bar. Before leaving, he decided to head into the bathroom and wash up. Not just because he needed to go, but also because it gave him one more opportunity to watch Heath before leaving entirely. On Darren's way out of the bathroom and to the front door of the wine store, he strolled by the bar again and just watched the man from a distance. The salad plate now stood empty, pushed off to the side again while he made notes on the newspaper as he'd done before. His eyes darted back and forth between the television and the newspaper. It seemed a bit old fashioned that someone even looked at the newspaper anymore, much less made notes on it. Then Heath stopped what he was doing, picked up his phone, and thumbed in a long text message.

The behavior was odd, to say the least, but nothing about the man sent up warning signals in Darren's mind. The man seemed to be honest enough to believe what he'd been telling Darren. No sweating, no nervous behavior except when he'd gotten the phone call from the unknown number. That bit was strange but didn't point toward issues with Liz that Darren could see.

He shrugged and continued out the door to his

sedan. The bright sun beat down on the vineyard from a cloudless, deep blue sky. Darren imagined the guests on the tour would be breaking a sweat from the direct sunlight even though the temperature was comfortable and there was a light breeze.

After sparing one last glance around at the property, Darren sighed. He just kept meeting dead end after dead end in this case. None of the pieces of the puzzle were fitting together easily. He guessed he'd have to just close the case after all, no matter that it made his gut feel queasy. Once he let out a deep breath, he ducked into his sedan. His cell rang. Unknown number. His mind flashed back to what Heath had said, and he half-expected the possibility of spam when he answered, "Hello, this is Detective Willis."

"Detective, this is John Farmer from We Tow All. Animal control has taken the snake out of the SUV and searched the vehicle for more. We've given it a once over and found no issues with it except tires that are heading a little bit toward bald that we suggest the owner consider changing them soon." The voice on the other line was slightly nasally and monotone.

A smile tugged at Darren's lips. "Thank you. I'll

let the owner know that she can come get her truck."

"Thank you, detective."

When he'd hung up the phone, Darren dialed Felicity right away. There was no answer, but instead of leaving a message, Darren decided to text her since he was still sitting in the parking lot to let her know that her SUV was ready for pick up. He then sent her a second text, offering to give her a ride to the towing company, if she needed. He smiled down at his phone. She hadn't yet answered his messages, but just the thought that she'd be looking at them sent butterflies dancing through his stomach. He started his engine and left the winery, heading to the hotel to work on the robbery case.

Chapter Twelve
―――――――――――

FELICITY'S HEART skipped a beat when she saw Darren's unmarked sedan pulling from the long driveway of the winery and out onto the main highway. She waved, but he didn't see her. Because she was in Georgia's car instead of her own, she understood that he may not have recognized her so easily, but it didn't stop her stomach from dropping a little bit in disappointment.

Her heart stuttered the whole drive up to the winery and pounded harder when she pulled into a parking spot in the lot. A group of people were gathered on the covered porch area for a tasting. She frowned in disappointment. Staying outside of the building would be an impossibility. She picked up her phone and saw that she had both a missed call and two text messages from Darren.

Somehow, her ringer had been left off. She frowned and turned up the ringer on her phone and read the messages. Once finished, she shot a response over to Darren thanking him for the offer and asking what a good time would be for him to pick her up later in the afternoon. Then she called the lawyer back again.

"Hello?" his gruff voice asked on the other end of the line when he answered.

"Hi, Mr. Wright. I'm here at the winery. Where do you want me to meet you?"

"I'm in the main office. To get here, go past the wine store over to building directly behind it. It looks like a large, white, temporary trailer. It's where Elizabeth put her office space temporarily while they were expanding the winery."

Felicity took a deep breath. She considered asking if he could meet her at her car but thought better of it. No. The last thing she wanted to do was let fear take control of what she did or didn't do. "Okay. I'll meet you there in a moment."

After hanging up the phone, she stepped out of the two-door coup and called Jay to hop over the seat and join her. She pulled the leather leash from her pocket and snapped it onto his collar. His tail wagged as he spied all the people on the covered porch. Felicity scratched him behind the ears and then commanded him to sit.

She made certain her doors were locked this time before closing the doors. Her heart fluttered in her chest. Fear. She did her best to swallow it down, steel her spine, and follow the path around to the back of the winery where Mr. Wright awaited her. At least there was no ATV around that she could see, and no sign of Mr. Page.

"Felicity!" a deep voice called to her, and she turned a bit to find Heath Anderson jogging toward her from the area of the wine store.

"Hello," she called back, her hands fisting on the leash.

"I didn't expect to see you again today. I'm glad you're here though. Would you like to join one of the tours for a walk and tasting?"

She couldn't help but scrunch her brow at the offer. "Thank you, but I'm not sure if I'll have time. I'm only here to sign a few things for Mr. Wright, and then I'll be heading right back out again."

He nodded, a touch of disappointment as he pursed his lips, but that expression disappeared quickly, replaced with a smile. "If you haven't had lunch yet, you can join me at the bar. You have to eat, right?"

"I suppose, but I'm in a bit of a hurry, so I don't think I can even spare a moment for a sandwich."

"Ahh. I'll just have to spend another lonely meal on my own. If you change your mind, I'll be in at the bar." He waved and started back toward the wine store.

Felicity waved back and continued past several stacks of wine barrels and to the office at the end of the path she was walking. Once she let Jay lead her up the steps to the office, she opened the door for them both. The white trailer had brown trim on the outside, and a handicap ramp as well as stairs to the main entrance. From what she'd seen, it was similar to the portable office they'd bring to construction sites, only this one looked like it had been in this location for quite a while.

Air conditioning blasted cool air her direction as she entered. The main desk was slightly to Felicity's side, and Mr. Wright grinned up on her once she came in. "Lovely to see you, Miss Stilton."

"Thank you. Nice to see you, as well." She bowed her head slightly toward him and then sat in the chair across from him as he gestured.

"Your mother's business has been pretty much

handled. Virtually all of her assets are transferred directly to you. She has no other heirs or assigns. I believe that there are a few of the employees here who may be surprised at that turn of events, but I know that Elizabeth was an excellent businesswoman and wouldn't make that decision lightly." He handed her a pen and then turned a large bound checkbook her direction.

She peered at the green colored checks and saw that each one had notes to the side of them on a tab. Each check had been completely written out to the phone company, electric company, and other typical bills, as well as to the funeral home. A pinprick of sadness stabbed her in the heart as she looked at the last check. Tomorrow would be Liz's funeral, and she'd be saying goodbye to the woman she'd always wanted to get to know but had never had the opportunity. The loss of what-could-have-been weighed heavily on her heart. Tears stung the backs of her eyes, but she swallowed them down, took the pen Mr. Wright had offered her, and began signing.

"Unless you have any major changes to make here at the winery, Mr. Page and Mr. Anderson can easily handle things as they have always been. I'm happy to continue as your representative here and call you whenever there is something that needs your attention. After everyone is paid and the books are balanced, you'll receive a small check of income at the end of each month, but it will vary depending on the time of year and the amount the winery profits."

Once she'd finished signing the checks, Felicity looked up at Mr. Wright and listened intently.

"Curtis and Heath are reliable workers and good supervisors. They have a bit of a yin and yang... good cop, bad cop... thing going on between the two of them. The only real worry you have until you decide whether you will keep the winery or sell it is what is to be done with the main house. It's just under two thousand square feet and four bedrooms. It could be made into a bunkhouse for the migrant workers, or you could allow some of the other employees to live there if you're not interested in living there yourself."

Felicity frowned and cleared her throat, rubbing her arms from the chill of the air inside the trailer. "I'm not yet prepared to make any decision on whether to sell the winery... or what to do with the house. Could I have a week or two to think things over? I'd rather discuss these things with my adoptive parents when they return from their overseas trip."

As he swung the check book back around to face his direction, Mr. Wright nodded and then checked the signatures on each one of them individually as if to check Felicity's handwriting. "That's certainly understandable and doable. Everything here looks good. I guess we'll see each other again tomorrow for the funeral and the wake. The employees have asked that we have the wake here, in Liz's home after the funeral. I've taken the liberty of asking Miss Kim to prepare the house if that's okay?"

A lump lodged in Felicity's throat. She wasn't sure how she felt about dozens of strangers gathering in Liz's home. Then she remembered that they weren't strangers to Liz, and she nodded. "I think Liz would like that."

"Great. Then we'll see you at the funeral in the morning."

She nodded, the lump in her throat keeping her from saying another word about it. Though she felt distant from her birthmother, and that distance made it so that she didn't feel the kind of distraught sorrow that one would feel at her mother's death, sadness still gripped her insides. Part of it was the sadness she felt at the loss of anyone that she knew who died, even when it was just an acquaintance. But also, there was a feeling of emptiness from the knowledge that Liz was her mother and she was gone.

After shaking hands with Mr. Wright, Felicity led Jay to the door and back outside. The sun shone down on her from overhead, warming up her skin so that it prickled slightly. She closed her eyes as the door shut behind her and just lifted her face toward it and let the rays flood over her.

"Glad to see you finally listened about putting that dog on a leash."

She choked and coughed as her eyes snapped open. Her gaze shot toward the sound of the voice she'd heard. Curtis Page sat in his ATV, leaning on the steering wheel as she stood on the top step of the trailer office. The fear she'd felt earlier returned, and her stomach flipped. But she refused to allow the fear to get a foothold. She battled it the best way she knew how—with anger. She glared at the man as she walked down the steps to the path below. "Good afternoon to you, too, Mr. Page."

He returned her glare with a scowl. "Good afternoon."

They had a momentary staring contest of her

walking past him and him dismounting his ATV, and then she turned her nose away and allowed JJ to lead her back toward the parking lot. As she rounded the stacks of barrels, a creaking sound drew her attention, and the sound of cracking wood.

"Look out!" Mr. Page shouted from behind her.

For a moment, she couldn't tell what she was looking at. The barrels at the top of the stack seemed to move backward, away from her, but then she found the barrels at the bottom were rolling in her direction.

She felt rough hands push her out of the way as the first of the barrels rolled past where she'd just been standing. Four more joined in. She blinked and found Mr. Page standing overtop of her. "Why on earth would you just stand there and watch the barrels coming to you? Do you have a death wish or something?"

Ringing filled her ears as her anger bubbled up more. She drew herself to her feet and dusted herself off. Jay whined up at her. "No, I don't have a death wish. But it seems you might be trying to kill me!"

His eyes grew wide for a moment. "What are you talking about?"

She gestured toward the barrels. "You made this happen, didn't you?"

The scowl came back to his face, full-force. "Are you crazy? Why on earth would I do that?"

"You're trying to hurt me because I'm Liz's daughter, aren't you? You killed her and made it look like a suicide, and now you're trying to kill me. I don't know what grudge you had against my mother, but I don't want anything to do with this winery. I just want to live in peace." Felicity hadn't realized that she'd been shouting until she noticed that they'd had an audience. Mr. Wright stood on the porch of the office trailer, while Mr. Anderson and three of the purple-shirted staff stood next to the main building.

Heat rushed up her neck and warmed her face as she blushed.

"I would never hurt Liz. I would never hurt you. I just saved you from being crushed by these barrels. They are filled with a salt solution for storage, and each one weighs over six-hundred pounds. Why would I push you out of the way if I wanted to kill you?"

Felicity shook her head and gripped Jay's leash harder. "Last minute act of conscience?"

He shook his head, his eyes going a little wide again.

"Darren knows that this is a murder. He's been looking into it. It's only a matter of time before he finds the evidence that puts you away." Felicity hoped her poker face was convincing, because she just upped the ante with nothing but a bluff.

Mr. Page shook his head harder, like a dog would when trying to get water out of its coat. "I don't need to stand here and listen to this. I've got better things to do."

Felicity stood there, breathing heavily for a moment, staring at Mr. Page's back as he headed to his ATV and peeled out.

"Are you okay, Felicity?" Heath Anderson stood next to her and rested a hand lightly on her shoulder. His brows knit over his worried-looking eyes.

As nice as he was being, Felicity just wanted to be alone. She slipped to the side. "Thank you. I'm fine. I'm sorry for causing a scene," she said, and then ducked her head and started toward Georgia's car in the lot.

Once she'd unlocked the door and let herself in, she swiped the tears from her eyes that had blurred her vision. It had happened again. Another accident. Too many accidents to just be coincidental.

Curtis Page wanted her dead, she was certain. She shook her head and grabbed her phone, wanting to call Darren and tell him everything that had just happened. But at the same time, she didn't want to feel the rejection his dismissal would cause. She took a deep breath and let it out slowly, and then noticed a text message from Darren.

Pick you up at your house at about four?

It was almost two-thirty right now. That gave her enough time to get back home and hop in the shower again before he came. She sent a quick text back: *Perfect.* And then started the car and headed home.

DARREN SAT across from Felicity at one of the few chain restaurants in town. He had been happy she'd accepted his dinner invitation after they'd stopped to pick up her SUV, because he could tell there was something eating away at her. Now that he'd heard the events of the afternoon, his stomach sank and so did his mood.

"I'm really sorry to hear that. You're right. The chances of there being three accidents at the winery in the past two days that could have taken your life are slim to none. It's more than a coincidence." Although Darren had been positive that the man seemed honest and hardworking—and not a murderer—maybe he'd been fooled.

"You still haven't closed the case yet?"

He shook his head. "I was supposed to today, but my lieutenant cut me some slack because I closed the case of the hotel robbery today."

She blinked, a smile spreading across her face. "You did? That's incredible! Congratulations."

Darren's hand went to the back of his neck and he rubbed it, looking down at the plate of pancakes stacked in front of him. Felicity had said she'd wanted breakfast for dinner, so they both had gotten eggs, pancakes, and sausages. But they'd been talking when their food arrived, and they hadn't yet tucked in. He smiled up at her sheepishly as he pulled the hand from the back of his neck and picked up his fork. "Thank you."

She followed his lead and picked up her fork as well. "Has it always been your dream to be a detective?"

He stabbed a sausage with his fork and then nodded before biting it in half. His kid brother, Tony, always got after him for talking with his mouth full, so he chewed and swallowed, pretending to think it over before speaking. "Yes. My uncle was a detective and I always looked up to him. My father was an auto-mechanic, so he was really happy to see me follow after his brother and get a job that didn't work with my hands and needed a bit more education."

"Didn't you go to UCLA?"

He nodded again. "I did, and Tony is going there right now."

She smiled wide. "Tony. Ugh. I haven't seen him since he was like… twelve."

"He's still a cute little troublemaker. He hasn't changed much since he was twelve… maybe he's a little taller."

"Those dimples though. I bet he's a heartbreaker."

Darren laughed. "Probably."

"You have one, too. He has dimples in both his cheeks, but you have one that pops when you smile. Does that make you half the heartbreaker he is?" Cute and clever. Felicity never let him rest, and he rather liked that about her.

He shrugged, swallowing down the bite of pancake he'd taken. "I don't know about that."

She nodded, eating a bit of her eggs. "What about Kent? Didn't he go to UCLA?"

Darren felt his face scrunch just a bit. "No. He actually did follow in my dad's footsteps a bit. He liked working with his hands more, so he went to Gold Coast Community College and got an Associate's Degree in Business so he didn't have to move away from Monique. Dad co-signed a loan for him so he could start his own garage. In that way, he works for himself, and that's what makes him happy."

"Wow, I'm embarrassed that Monique and I fell so out of touch that I didn't even know what was going on with the two of them."

He shook his head and grabbed a sip of his orange juice to wash down another bite. "Don't be embarrassed. It's amazing that the high school sweethearts are still together after all this time. So, how about you? Are you doing what you always wanted to do?"

She nodded. "I am. I always wanted to work with JJ to help children who have reading disabilities. It's a subject that's close to my heart, because I grew up with dyslexia." She blushed a bit and kept her eyes downcast at that last part.

Butterflies tickled Darren's stomach. She'd just shared something deeply personal to her with him, and he understood the significance of it. "That's great. Not only do you get to make sure that other children suffer less than you did, but you also get to work with your canine best friend on a daily basis."

She looked up and smiled. "Yes! You totally get it. People have one of two reactions when I tell them what I do: skepticism or cynicism—as if what I do is small and unnecessary… or just plain hokey. But I believe that children learn better when they have a non-judgmental partner helping them along the way. And JJ's the perfect partner."

"Sounds great and makes perfect sense. I know that those children are benefiting greatly from having both you and JJ in their lives. Where did you get him, by the way? Was he trained to be a therapy dog before you got him?"

"Oh, no. My parents got him for me for my birthday about three years ago. He comes from a line of working golden retrievers who all have jobs in therapy, obedience, and other lines of work. It's pretty incredible, but Carol Graves, the breeder, even sends email updates on how JJ's littermates are out there saving the world." Her eyes sparkled as she talked about her best friend. It was almost enough to make Darren jealous.

But he wasn't jealous. He understood. Dogs were practically heaven-sent. He'd had the best dog of his whole life as a teenager—one that had helped him through his mother's death. He'd been heartbroken when it, too, died of cancer. They just didn't live long enough. If the world was just, dogs would live thirty or forty years or more.

The two of them fell into a comfortable silence as they finished their meal. Afterward, they took a stroll down the main street, back toward the lot where they'd parked their cars. A breeze blew back Felicity's ponytail, exposing her elegant neck and pale skin. She looked in the windows of each storefront as they passed—the bakery, a clothing store, a bookstore. It didn't matter what kind of store it was; Felicity gave each window her complete attention.

Which was fine, until she tripped over nothing, and Darren caught her to keep her from landing on the concrete. His hands remained on her elbows when she laughed at herself and said, "whoopsie," in the most adorable way.

Darren lifted an eyebrow at her and then placed her hand in his. "Lean on me for balance. I don't know if I've ever met a clumsier girl. Maybe you are just accident-prone."

She surprised him by squeezing his hand and punching him in the shoulder. "I'm clumsy, but there's no way I tripped myself into a cooler or a rattlesnake into my car."

His shoulder stung a little from where she'd hit it, but he didn't mind it. It was an affectionate tap, and it distracted him from how much he liked the warmth of her hand in his. "Just kidding," he offered.

After shaking her head and rolling her eyes, she went back to window shopping on the way to the parking lot. It slowed down their walk, and he wondered for half a moment if that might be her goal. Did she not want this moment to end any more than he did? The thought of it brought those butterflies back to the pit of his stomach. Even though they hadn't made it official, was this their first date, in fact?

"Do you ever think about getting married?" she asked.

He blinked, nearly choking on the last breath he'd just drawn. "W-what?"

She pointed at the wedding dresses in the Hidden Gem bridal shop. "I'm not sure if I want to wear something fancy like that. When I think about all the work that goes into the wedding, I wonder if it's just easier to elope. That's what my parents did, and they had a successful marriage."

The dress in the window was extravagant with puffed-out sleeves, lace trim, and pearl-like beads everywhere. He swallowed and kept his eyes focused on the dress as he answered, "That does seem pretty fancy. But eloping means that your parents and family miss out on seeing the moment when you make that promise to love and honor someone for the rest of your life. I would want my dad and my brothers there. Family's important to me."

"I like that," she answered, smiling up at him when his eyes met hers. "You're right. Family is important. I'd want my mom and dad there, too. Maybe going through all the trouble of a wedding wouldn't be too bad, provided that it's small. Maybe even a backyard wedding."

Instead of letting him answer, she tugged his hand and moved on from the bridal shop. Why had his heart thundered so much in his chest when she'd talked about having a small wedding? Even though she hadn't said it would be their wedding, he couldn't help but imagine it for a brief moment. Felicity in a simpler but just as white dress, walking toward him down a grassy row between white folding chairs in a large yard like the winery. He swallowed those thoughts back down. Yes, he was falling hard for this girl, but marriage was not a topic he thought he'd discuss on a first date. As they continued on to the next shop, though, he couldn't get his heart to calm once more or his mind off the feeling of her hand in his.

When they reached their cars, parked side by side, he hesitated. He didn't want to let her hand go. She made no move to remove it herself. Every signal that she gave him was that she wanted to be with him as much as he wanted to be with her. Pink and purple washed through the sky as the sun began to set, and Felicity's eyes sparkled in the dying light. He couldn't help himself and leaned in toward her, smiling as she tilted her chin up and closed her eyes. Her hand squeezed his slightly.

He tasted her lips, the soft touch sending a jolt of electricity through his core. The feeling of her lips on his made him greedy, and he pulled her arm with his around her back, using both to draw her into his body. Her frame fit perfectly with his. And he kissed her again, feeling each lip separately between his. Her other hand fisted in the shirt on his back. His free hand felt the softness of her cheek in his palm. And he pulled away just enough to rest his forehead against hers. His eyes remained closed for a moment as he just breathed her in and savored the moment.

When he opened his eyes again, her bright blue irises had become a darker, midnight blue. He wondered at the sight and imagined all the shades of blue that they could be. He wanted to see them all. Slowly he pulled back and loosened his hold on her. He'd never thought about marriage or being with a girl forever like this, but Felicity brought out those feelings in him. Nothing about those thoughts with her scared him. They excited him instead.

She squeezed his hand and then pulled it away. "Goodnight," she said, her voice a little bit husky, a little bit breathless.

And the desire to catch her, pull her back in, and kiss her again overwhelmed him, but instead, he squeezed his empty hand into a fist to feel the memory of her warmth there again, and said, "Goodnight."

Chapter Thirteen

FELICITY LEANED hard on Georgia throughout the funeral, holding hands with her best friend. Georgia's red hair was pulled back in a bun from her face, and her mascara ran from the sides of her eyes while people spoke about their love and respect for Liz. Both Felicity's throat and stomach hurt from crying as much as she did, too. It was the first time that she truly felt that she was in mourning for her birthmother but releasing all those tears gave her the first closure she'd had since Darren had shown up in her driveway. Jay was her other stalwart companion, quietly sitting next to her through the whole event.

Together, they stepped up to Liz's house for the wake, finding Mr. Wright standing at the door, ready to shake hands with people as they came. Georgia promised to stay nearby as Felicity took her place next to him. Over and over again, she heard how no one had even known that Liz had a daughter, but how pretty Felicity was and how much she looked just like her mother. She smiled at everyone, shook hands, and accepted hugs from strangers. She began to feel numb from the constant contact and same repeated words. Even Jay couldn't get away from the constant pats or looks of wonder at why a dog would even be sitting on Liz's front porch.

After an hour or more of people coming, drinking wine, eating small sandwiches—because of course the event was catered by the winery—exhaustion overcame Felicity. She felt slightly dizzy, and Jay, who was always in tune with Felicity's emotional state, whined up at her. She patted him in reassurance but leaned in toward Mr. Wright. "I need to get away and just clear my head, and Jay's been sitting for a very long time. I think we both just need a walk."

"That's understandable. Do you want me to go with you or maybe your friend?"

Felicity peered into the house. Georgia was nowhere to be found. But she found Curtis Page.

Mr. Page had been sitting in one of the chairs by the fireplace, staring at all the pictures of Liz. As long as he stayed in the same place, she'd be safe on a short walk through the field and back. She wished Darren had been there, but he'd texted her a half-hour before the funeral to let her know that he wouldn't be there, and that he'd try to make the wake but not look for him. She sighed. His presence would have made the whole thing a little more bearable.

"It's okay. I'm fine." She smiled up at him, though it was weak.

The leather leash felt a bit awkward in her hand as Jay tugged at it, letting her know he wanted to be free. They were in an open area, and there was nothing he desired more than to run free and romp through the grass. Once they were a good distance from the house, Felicity unhooked the leash. The sky overhead was a faded shade of blue with the slightest bit of haze. Wispy clouds blocked out a modicum of sunshine.

The winery certainly was beautiful and close to nature as well as the city. The mountains were nearby, and so was the ocean. Wide open fields of nothing but grapevines and grass allowed for a panoramic view. She could see why Liz loved this place so much. Loved it more than anything. Loved it even more than having a daughter.

Finally, Felicity was being honest with herself. It hurt. It hurt that no one in Liz's life even knew she existed. It hurt that her birthmother had ever given her up in the first place in order to run this place. It hurt that even after she caught up with Liz as an adult, the woman could barely be bothered to get to know her. And now it hurt that Liz was gone and they'd never get to know each other.

Depression spiraled around Felicity, bringing up fresh sobs. Her heart felt as though made of lead—heavy in her chest. Then, as if whispered on the wind, one word reached her heart, in Liz's voice. Gratitude.

Felicity blinked and swiped at the tears in her eyes. The weight in her chest lightened the slightest bit. The parents she had were marvelous and gave her every opportunity that she needed growing up. Because of them, she was able to pursue any and every dream she had. She had the best job in the world. Even though it felt tenuous at times, all she needed to do was prove herself, and she knew she would. Then there was Georgia. She couldn't have asked for a better friend and roommate. Georgia was always there for her whenever she needed her.

Jay jumped after a butterfly, proving that even at three years old, he still had puppy moments. Felicity laughed, even though tears still welled in the bottom of her eyelids. She swiped them away again. Jay was a huge blessing in her life; not only did she get to work with him and help children, but he always offered unconditional love and companionship.

Then her heart fluttered when she thought of Darren.

At the same moment she lost Liz, she gained Darren. Her first crush was fast becoming her first love. She'd dated a bit in college but felt nothing for them like she'd always felt for Darren, even in high school. Now the one man she would have written off as an impossible dream had come into her life as a very real possibility. She remembered the feeling of his lips on hers, and found her fingers lightly touching her lips at the thought.

Liz had been right. There was nothing like gratitude to chase away the spiraling thoughts of depression. Maybe Liz did struggle with bouts of depression, but she'd found a way that worked for her to pull her out of it by thinking on the things that made her life happy and worth living instead of the empty shells of what could have been.

"There you are," a deep voice behind her

called, and for a moment, her heart fluttered as she hoped it might be Darren.

But when she turned around, Heath Anderson stood in front of her, a pistol in his hand. She blinked, her heart dropping to her stomach. Her gaze shot around him to see if anyone else was coming, but the house was hidden by a row of grapevines.

"Don't bother. If you scream for help, I'll shoot you and the dog."

Bile rose in her throat. How could she possibly scream past the lump that had formed there? Her eyes searched his. What was going on? His face was lined and hard. Nothing about it seemed the opening, welcoming, soft one she'd grown used to in past few days. It was contorted with hatred, and his eyes were icy cold.

"You ruined everything." His voice started out as a harsh whisper but grew louder as he spoke. "Lizzy didn't have family. No parents, no brothers and sisters, no children. She never spoke of you or anyone else. This place was supposed to be mine. *MINE*."

He waved the gun her direction and took a quick step toward her. Felicity stepped back in response. His hair was disheveled, and his necktie pulled down to let the top button of his shirt free. He looked crazy. But still she didn't understand. Why was he doing this?

"I could have paid off all my debts and gotten a fresh start here. I could have started that bed and breakfast that Lizzy always scoffed at. But no. You came in and ruined everything. *EVERYTHING.*"

Another stomp forward. Felicity retreated again. She wanted to turn around and run as his words began to click in place, and slowly things were making sense. The cooler. She'd only gone in there because he'd told her to. And he'd never said anything about there being a trick to opening the door again. He was the one who told her that Mr. Page was the snake lover, but could that have been a lie? Was he setting up the groundskeeper to take the fall after putting the snake in her car? And she had seen him before going in for the meeting with Mr. Wright. Was it possible that Heath had set the wine barrels up to fall when she came back out?

Her heart hammered in her chest. "You killed Liz."

His eyes narrowed. "You're just figuring that out now? Blondes really are dense. Your detective boyfriend already has things figured out. He's already giving me looks as though he knows. He's just looking for the last bits of evidence to put the nails in my coffin, but I'm not going to let that happen. You're coming with me."

Heath unceremoniously leapt toward her and grabbed her by the arm. The smallest cry escaped her lips, and he punched her in the cheek. "Shut up. I mean it, or I'll kill both you and the dog."

Pain blossomed in her face. She whimpered, her eyes flitting toward Jay who looked up at them with a confused expression. And then Heath began dragging her deeper into the vineyard, and Jay followed.

DARREN PULLED up to the vineyard parking lot and ended up parking in the grass along the driveway, as the lot itself was too full. Liz's death had an impact on several people in the community, and many came out to her wake to show their love and support for the memory of the woman who had touched their lives. He remembered the people who'd come out to his mother's funeral and how their fondness for his mother had been a small comfort to him. He hoped that Felicity found comfort in the memories of those who attended the wake.

Finding Felicity

He got out of his car and adjusted his tie. He had never grown accustomed to wearing a suit, but felt it was the most appropriate dress for the wake that he'd almost missed because of the embezzlement case he'd been working. But the interrogation worked, and he'd found an inconsistency in the suspect's story that allowed him to then break the truth out of him. The lieutenant actually patted him on the back as he booked the suspect.

Everything was falling into place at work; he'd solved two cases in the past two days, and so the lieutenant had left him alone about Liz Collier's death. Darren just didn't feel comfortable closing the folder on it as a suicide when so much evidence pointed to it being something more sinister.

The gravel under his feet crunched as he headed up toward the house. Early afternoon sunlight felt good against the back of his navy blue blazer. Lucian Wright stood at the front door of the house, saying good-bye to a couple who was coming out. Darren felt bad he'd missed the funeral. He really wanted to be there for Felicity, and though he was late for the wake, he decided to come and lend any support for her that he could.

He stepped to the side and allowed the couple

to come down from the steps before he ascended them himself.

"Detective. Good of you to come." Mr. Wright had a wide smile on his face and offered a hand to shake.

Darren took the hand and squeezed it. "Good of you to be the greeter for Liz on Felicity's behalf. Do you know where I can find her?"

As they released hands, the older man shrugged. "A little while ago, she'd said she'd take the dog for a short walk and get a breath of fresh air. But I think she came back already? I'm not sure. Why don't you check inside first?"

He nodded and headed in the doorway. The room was filled with people standing around and talking to one another in hushed tones, but still the low mumble was a bit overwhelming as his mind couldn't quite grab hold of any particular conversation. When he spied Curtis Page sitting on a chair in the living room, hugging a glass of wine to his chest and looking up at a picture of Liz, he decided to sit on the sofa across from the lonely looking old man.

When he sat down, Curtis blinked and looked his direction. Then in embarrassment, the older man swiped the tears that had welled in the bottoms of his eyes.

And a thought dawned in Darren's mind. "You loved her."

Curtis's eyes grew wide a moment, and he shook his head vigorously. Then the momentum died as though the man weakened, and he looked down at the floor and nodded. "I did, but I never told her. I never let her know. For the past few years she'd been with that leech, Anderson. And it felt like I could never get close enough to her after that. I had hoped, now that they'd broken up, to give her time to get over the man before making my confession."

Felicity had been wrong. There was no way this man would have killed the woman he loved right when he was getting ready to confess his feelings for her. But something else about what the man said bothered him. "You called Heath a leech?"

The man's face puckered up like he'd just eaten a lemon. He lifted his wine glass and took a quick sip before meeting Darren's eyes with his own drunken ones. "A gambler. He was always pushing Liz to do something new and different with the winery, when things were working just fine as they were. His changes would always cost tons of money and who knew if they'd work out." His hand gestured to the room. "He wanted to tear down this house and build a bigger one so that they could start a bed and breakfast. Do you know how much money that would cost?"

Darren shrugged. Business decisions like that were always a gamble, and one needed to spend money to make money. He didn't know how successful that change would be, but it did seem a bit extreme to discuss tearing down a perfectly good house and structure, just to build a bigger one.

"He stole from her," Curtis whispered.

That got Darren's attention. "What do you mean?"

The older man leaned in toward him. "She'd been missing jewelry and silverware—small but valuable things. He blamed the housekeeper, but Mrs. Park had been cleaning Liz's house for more than eight years. Why would she suddenly steal from her? Yes, Mrs. Park had some hospital bills that seemed to coincide with when things went missing, but I just don't believe it. The Asian woman was smart and loyal, but she didn't even defend herself when Heath made his accusation. That's why Liz let her go."

Darren shook his head. "Why would he steal from her?"

"Gambling debts. He didn't just want to gamble with Liz's business. He's always on the phone with his bookie. Betting on every sports event—every horse race."

Blood drained from Darren's face. He remembered how Heath had been watching horseracing during lunch and then showed disappointment in the results. Had he ignored the phone call while Darren was there because it was his bookie? Gambling was legal in the state of California, but only on the horse racing. If Heath Anderson was betting on other sports events, too, he was breaking the law.

"He killed her. I know he killed my Liz. I just don't know why… I just don't have any evidence to prove it." Curtis's words began to slur. He must have been drinking for more than an hour if he started when the wake began. Darren eyed the old man. Chances were that Mr. Page had started drinking even earlier than that. He couldn't take what the man said as fact, but his statements did bring up a lot of questions and the possibility of a motive.

Darren's eyes moved around the room. He

didn't see Heath Anderson anywhere, but then his eyes lighted on a face he did recognize. Georgia, Felicity's roommate. He stood and headed her direction by the staffed bar. She was talking with the bartender and laughing as though the two of them knew one another. When he reached her, her gaze fluttered his direction, and he offered a wide smile. "Hi, Georgia. You may not know me, but I'm Detective Darren Willis."

Her own smile grew as she looked him up and down, while the ice in her club soda jingled. "Of course. It's a pleasure to meet you, detective."

His hand reached for the back of his neck and he rubbed it there as he blushed a little. "I'm looking for Felicity. Have you seen her?"

She peered around the room, past him and over toward the entrance. Her eyes scrunched a little as though she was short-sighted and not wearing her glasses. "She's not by the front door? She's been there the whole time."

He shook his head. "So, she didn't come inside after taking JJ for a walk?"

Georgia shook her head. "I haven't seen her."

Darren frowned, dread filling his stomach with an icy cold. He searched the room again for Heath Anderson, but couldn't find the tall, smarmy man anywhere. If Mr. Page was right and Heath had killed Liz, then it was also possible he was behind the "accidents" that had plagued Felicity the past few days. And now she was missing, and he was nowhere to be found. Darren didn't like this, and he darted for the front door.

Chapter Fourteen

"WHY ARE YOU DOING ALL THIS?" Felicity asked, hating the whininess in her voice. But fear had taken a firm hold on her heart this time, and she wasn't able to replace it with anger yet. He'd dragged her through the field for over twenty minutes, putting more and more distance between her and the house.

"She broke up with me. That wench figured out I'd been stealing from her, not the housekeeper. The likelihood of her firing me when I got back from the Napa convention was too great. I was poised to lose everything. But I could get it all back and more if I just took it from her. The business was struggling a few years ago; it only started doing better because I came along and helped it. I deserved it all, and she was going to take it all away from me." His tugs on her arm became more violent as he dragged her farther into the field.

"Where are you taking me?"

He chuckled. "Did you know that at the edge of the property, there's a path that Liz lets people traverse as part of the Cliff Walk? This property has the best view, and it would go to waste if those people didn't come by at certain times of the day and walk along the edge and look at the ocean."

She frowned. What did that have to do with anything?

He looked down at her and narrowed his eyes. "I'd just really like for you to see it."

She shook her head. That was crazy—she almost said it, but bit down on her lower lip to stop herself from provoking him further. Then Heath tripped, his hand on her arm pulling her down with him. Her arm broke free from his grip, and the gun skittered away in the grass a few feet from his hands. She didn't let this opportunity go to waste. After scrambling back to her feet, she made a run for it. Her arms pumped as her feet hit the ground and for a moment the ringing in her hears subsided, and she noticed something was missing. She ran everyday with Jay, listening the quiet jingle of his tag against the metal of his collar, but that sound was missing. Her feet slowed as her joints locked up. She looked back.

Jay wasn't with her.

Her heart sank. Why hadn't he followed?

For a moment, she panted, trying to catch her breath, trying to keep the tears from falling. But Jay still didn't come.

Then she heard Heath's voice. "Felicity! Are you really going to leave your precious golden behind? I thought he meant more to you than that."

Her vision blurred as the tears filled her eyes. "What do you want?" she screamed at the top of her lungs, but they had to be more than a half-mile from the house. Could anyone hear her?

"I just need to talk with you and get you to sign a check for me. That's all, and then I'll let you go." His voice sounded calm and rational.

Even though she'd put several yards of distance between her and him, his voice carried over the tops of the vines around the bend. She shook her head. That couldn't be all he wanted. A gun wouldn't be necessary if that was all he wanted. Why would he need to drag her all the way out here?

She took a step back toward the house, but her

heart wrenched in her chest at the thought of leaving Jay. His soft brown eyes appeared in her mind, and she couldn't bear the thought of losing him. Her feet stopped. There was no way that she could lose him.

"Let's go." His voice was closer, and when Felicity turned around, she could see him on the bend, holding Jay's collar. Jay continued to smile and pant with his mouth open, completely unaware of the danger he was in.

The tears streamed down Felicity's face, and a sob escaped her lips.

Heath pointed the gun at her. "No need for all that. Just walk with me."

Her feet propelled her toward him even though she didn't want to go. It was too late to run now; he had her in his sights and could shoot her if she ran. And he'd already promised to kill Jay, too.

Once she was in his reach, he backhanded her with his pistol hand. Pain shot through her face on the opposite side of where she'd already been punched. Stars exploded in her vision, and she fell to the ground, the back of her head slamming against the ground.

A growl, snarl, and a shout reached her ears.

She couldn't open her right eye, but when she

opened her left, she found Jay had grabbed hold of Heath's arm and shook it like a guard dog. Her left eye opened wider in surprise. Jay had never shown aggressive behavior toward anyone.

Heath punched the golden several times in the side before Jay finally let go. Then he pointed his pistol at the dog.

"No!" she screamed as the man pulled the trigger.

"SO, you haven't seen her anywhere?" Darren asked the lawyer on the porch again.

He shrugged. "I thought for sure she came back from her walk with the dog, but I might have been mistaken."

Darren's frown deepened. "Which way did she go?"

Lucian Wright scratched his chin a moment and then pointed in the direction of the vine fields. "That way."

Then the pop of a gunshot made the hairs on the back of Darren's neck stand on end. The sound had come from the direction the lawyer was pointing. Lucian's eyes widened at the sound, and

Darren's hand went to the handle of his pistol. He dashed down the steps of the porch and called back toward the lawyer. "Call 9-1-1 and tell them an officer needs assistance."

"Okay!" Mr. Wright called back, but Darren didn't look over his shoulder to see; he was already running in the direction of gunfire as fast as his legs would take him.

JAY WOULDN'T STOP CRYING. Felicity had never heard him scream so much as he tried to stand and couldn't. She wanted to go to him and comfort him. Red blossomed in the golden fur around his hind leg. But Heath Anderson already had a hold of her arm again and was dragging her with him. Her right eye still wouldn't open, and she felt the swelling grow.

He yanked her harder and pushed her to the ground in front of him. He pointed his pistol at her. The sleeve of his blazer was torn, exposing the white shirt and a trace of blood red. "Do you want to die, Felicity. I can kill you now if you want."

She shook her head, sobs racking her body so she couldn't speak. "Please," she said, but it sounded incomprehensible and blubbery to her own ears. She just wanted to get back to Jay and comfort him. His cries were subsiding, becoming less frequent. Was he dying?

"Then get up. Let's go."

She scrambled to her feet, felt the cold metal of the gun in her back as he shoved her forward again. They continued walking for a few minutes more when the cliffs came into sight. It could have been a beautiful view, but she could only see it through the veil of her tears, and through only one eye.

The breeze picked up off the water and blew harder around them. Heath shoved her closer to the rocks on the edge, and then caught her arm with his hand, dangling her over the cliff.

Finally, she was able to form words. "Why are you doing all this?"

"I just want what's mine. Liz wouldn't give it to me, so you are. Here." He pulled a green piece of paper from his pocket and a pen and shoved them both her direction. "Sign that."

Confused, she took the paper from him and opened it up. It was a check for forty-seven thousand dollars, made out to his name. She blinked at it and then back up at him.

"Sign it. Now." He shoved her to the ground, so she was sitting on the rocks of the cliff.

The check fluttered in between her fingers in the breeze. And for a moment she had a crazy thought. What if she—

"Let that go and I will shoot you. I swear to God, I'll shoot you," he hissed.

She clenched her teeth and shook her head, tightening her fingers grip on the check. What did it matter? Was that what Liz's life was worth? What Jay's life was worth? Forty-seven thousand dollars? She'd gladly have written him the check if he would just leave her alone. Did he really need to go through all this for the money?

"Get on with it," he shouted over the wind.

"Fine," she yelled back and then pushed the check against the rocks and placed her signature on the bottom. Once finished, she offered him the check, and he snatched it from her fingers.

A sickening smile spread across his lips.

She glared up at him. "Are you happy now? Good. Can I go?"

He grabbed her by the elbow and pulled her up to her feet. The look in his eye became sinister. "I know I promised to let you go after you wrote the check, but I didn't say how."

Then he wrenched her body back by the arm, so she nearly lost her footing. He leaned her body over the cliff, and no matter how much she struggled, she couldn't right herself.

DARREN'S LUNGS BURNED. He'd been running for more than half a mile and hadn't reached the source of the gunshot yet. What if he was going the wrong way? What if the gunshot had been two degrees to the left or the right when he'd heard it? He may have even passed Felicity already. The thought of her hurt and bleeding in one of the other vine rows made him sick to his stomach.

Then he heard whimpering.

After rounding the next bend, the golden retriever came into view. Though dragging his bloody hind end along the grass, he was heading away from the house and toward the cliffs. He was still trying to get to Felicity.

It wasn't Felicity who was shot. It was JJ. Though Darren's heart broke, knowing that the dog had been hurt, he couldn't help but feel a moment of relief. He stopped next to JJ and knelt to pat him on the head. "You're a good boy. It's okay. I'll get her. She's going to be all right."

The dog looked up at him, smiling, panting, pausing for a moment in his struggle to drag himself toward his owner. Darren wanted to help the poor thing but needed to get to Felicity. He stood, and before he could even take a step forward, the dog renewed his efforts. Darren shook his head. He didn't know what to do. Should he end the dog's suffering?

Then he heard the hum of an engine as an ATV rounded the corner between the rows of vines. Curtis Page. Darren smiled up at him. "Curtis! Can you take JJ back toward the house? He's been shot and needs to see the vet."

Mr. Page blinked several times. Then he answered, "Yes. Should I carry him? You want to take the ATV?"

Darren shook his head. Felicity would want JJ saved, and the golden retriever deserved it after taking a bullet. "Take the dog in the back of the ATV. I've got to go."

After seeing Curtis nod his head, Darren darted in the direction of the cliffs with new energy. He now knew he was heading the right direction and that Felicity wasn't the one who was shot. If he could make it in time to save her, that was all he needed.

FELICITY SCREAMED. "Why are you doing this?"

Heath frowned. "Stop sounding like a broken record. How many times have you asked me that question? Three? Four?"

She had no answer—the sobs had closed her throat to words again.

"I'm out of here. I'm cashing in this check and leaving town, but I can't have you telling everyone about what I did. If you're dead, no one will know that I've taken the money out of the account until it's too late. I can't have you putting a stop to it at the bank." His eyes had gone crazy.

The whole thing was crazy. How could anyone let themselves get this way? *Hurt people hurt others.* That's what her mother always said. In what way had Heath Anderson been hurt that he put so much emphasis on money as if it was the only thing he needed to make his life better? She swallowed, and the sobs subsided enough for her to say something. "Liz loved you."

He blinked at her, the brows over his forehead knitting. "What?"

"I read it in her journal. She didn't care about what you'd done and wanted to take you back. I didn't know what she was talking about at the time, but now I understand."

His arm relaxed a bit and stopped her lean toward the open air below. Her feet regained footing, and she was nearly upright. His eyes searched hers. "What do you mean?"

"Liz was grateful to you and for you. She talked about it in her journal. She understood that you did so much for her and deserved to be a part of her life."

"I asked her to marry me years ago, but she declined. She always declined." His hand loosened on her arm.

She nodded. "She was getting ready to accept."

That last part may have been an exaggeration. Liz's journal said nothing about marrying Heath, but right now Felicity needed for Heath to believe it did. She needed him to believe that Liz would have been willing.

Heath's hand released its hold on her entirely and went to his chest as though it ached. His gaze dropped to the rocks beneath their feet. "No. She couldn't have. I didn't just stop her from—" He staggered back a step.

His gaze trained up and met hers again, searching.

She kept her gaze steady on his but saw movement out of the corner of her one good eye. Her heart fluttered. Someone was coming their direction. She nodded her head. "It's true."

Tears filled the bottoms of Heath's eyelids as he staggered back another step. And then Darren tackled him, forcing the gun from Heath's hand as they wrestled on the ground together. Felicity bit her bottom lip and clenched her hands in worry. Please let Darren be okay in this. She needed him to be okay. She couldn't lose him too.

After a few moments of struggle, Darren sat up on Heath's back and wrenched the man's hands around to slap cuffs on him. His deep baritone suddenly sounded deeper as he said, "Heath Anderson, you're under arrest."

Relief flooded Felicity, and she collapsed to her knees in the grass on the edge of the cliff. Then her thoughts went toward Jay and she scrambled to her feet. Tears filled her eyes as she ran back up the vine row she'd come.

Chapter Fifteen

DARREN GRIPPED Felicity's hand in his lap as Dr. Keller, the veterinarian, came back into the waiting area. The older man smiled down at them. "Good news. The surgery was a success, as was the blood transfusion. He's recovering now."

Felicity collapsed in Darren's arms and hugged him tightly; another sob escaped her. She'd been doing a lot of crying throughout the two hours of surgery, and he was glad this time it wasn't tears of sadness or guilt but relief.

"Thank you, Doctor," Darren whispered over Felicity's head.

She pulled away and swiped her eyes, and then she drew to her feet. "Thank you so much, Dr. Keller. I really can't thank you enough."

He smiled. "JJ had lost a lot of blood, but luckily it was a small bullet, only a .22. It was also good that you all got him in here so quickly. I'd love to hear the story of how all this happened when you have the time. I love that JJ's now a hero."

Felicity smiled weakly. "He really is."

Darren stood and nodded, pulling Felicity back into his arms. Georgia smiled up at them from her seat. When Curtis had gotten back to the house in the ATV, he helped carry the golden retriever to Felicity's SUV. Georgia had the keys to the car, and she raced JJ to town and to the nearest vet. The bartender happened to navigate and now sat next to Georgia as well. Once he'd dropped off the dog with Georgia, Curtis Page returned to the cliff and found Felicity collapsed on the ground where the blood had pooled from JJ's injury.

He told her what had happened, helped her into the passenger seat of the two-seater ATV, and then continued down to find Darren and Heath walking back toward the house. He helped them both into the bed of the ATV, but not before landing one good punch in Heath's eye. "For Liz and her daughter," he'd said and then spat at the man.

"JJ will be spending the next hour or so in recovery before he's able to go home. There's no need for you to stay here and wait if you'd rather go get something for dinner," the veterinarian said, as though politely trying to get rid of the group that had been hanging out in his waiting area for the past few hours.

Darren got the hint and nodded to him. He pulled Felicity away from him. "Do you want to go get checked out at the hospital?"

Her eye was still swollen, and both sides of her face had taken on a purple hue. He wondered if the bone beneath the eye might be broken for the amount of swelling that sat underneath it.

But still, she shook her head stubbornly. "I'm fine. I'll just take an anti-inflammatory."

Dr. Keller cleared his throat. "Actually, I believe the detective is right. You should at least stop in at the emergency care clinic across the street. They may want to take an x-ray of your injury."

Felicity frowned but then looked up at Darren and nodded. Georgia came over and took Felicity's hand in both of hers. "Darling, I know you don't like to admit when there's something wrong with you, but right now you need to take care of yourself. JJ is okay. He's recovering. He needed to see the doctor and so do you."

A sigh escaped Felicity. "Fine."

Darren smiled and took a step back from the roommates, but when Georgia released her grip on Felicity's hands, Felicity immediately took hold of his arm again. He took comfort in it and let her pull him closer. The feeling of her warmth against him and the fact that she wanted him there were all that he needed to stay.

His phone vibrated in his pocket, and he pulled it out to check his text message. The police lieutenant was inviting him out for drinks to celebrate the closing of the winery case—the third successful close in Darren's first week as a detective. He texted back with one hand on the phone and the other wrapped around Felicity's shoulders.

Busy now. Will take a raincheck.

THE BONE in Felicity's cheek wasn't broken, but her eyelid had a major hematoma that needed draining, so she waited while the doctor drew blood from her eyelids. Once he was finished, she could happily open her right eye once more. Although the vision was a little blurry in that eye, and she had darkness around the edges, the doctor felt that it would heal on its own in a few days and prescribed her anti-inflammatories.

She was happy to take the prescription from the doctor and gave the receptionist her insurance information as they started toward the parking lot. Georgia leaned in and gave her a hug. "Peter and I are going to run ahead and grab a couple pizzas. We'll meet you back at the house after you pick up JJ."

Felicity smiled, her heart swelling with gladness that she wasn't mourning the loss of her beloved friend. Her eyes stung at the thought, but she felt as though the fountain of her tears had finally dried. She nodded to her roommate.

Darren squeezed her shoulders. As they passed his sedan and started toward the glass door of the vet's office, she caught sight of her reflection and gasped. She covered her face with her hands and turned away from Darren.

"What's wrong? Are you okay? Does it hurt?" Panic filled Darren's words.

"I'm hideous," she said into her palms, her voice muffled.

Above her, silence lasted for several seconds.

She feared for half a moment that he'd left. Then she turned toward him and peeked through her fingers. His soft eyes looked at her, filled with so much emotion that it took her breath away. They glistened with tears. His lips quivered as he said, "I'm so sorry."

She frowned but didn't move her hands away from her face.

"I should have been there sooner. He would never have hurt you or JJ if I had just been there." One of the tears broke free and slipped down his cheek.

She pulled her hands away and shook her head. "It's not your fault."

"And you're still beautiful."

She gasped again as her heart skipped a beat.

"You're still more beautiful than any girl I've ever seen. Even with your bruises and your swelling. I'm so glad you came back into my life." Tears continued to stream down his face.

He felt the same way about her that she did about him. Her heart soared, and she jumped toward him, wrapping her arms around his neck. "I'm happy that *you* came back into *my* life," she said into his chest.

When she pulled back a bit to look into his maple brown eyes, he smiled down at her and then kissed her. Their lips met, and the warmth of their love intermingled with the salt of their tears. Nothing had ever tasted so sweet.

Sneak Peek
_____

Read the first chapter of HELPING HANNA, book 6 of the Gold Coast Retrievers…

THE CLOCK on the church steeple towering above the town of Redwood Cove on the Gold Coast of California began its hourly song. Each chime matched Hanna's racing footsteps. One. Two. Three. Four. Five. Six. Seven.

She was late for work. Rushing wouldn't change that fact but she pressed on anyway. With several minutes to go before she arrived at the Cup of Joe Diner, Hanna wondered if she could sugarcoat this disaster. Rounding the corner at the side of the diner, she secured Bella in a shady spot. Brushing stray golden dog hairs from her black pants, and then gathering her thick auburn tresses into a ponytail, she headed through the door of the diner, straight into the glare of her boss, Joe Craven.

"Hanna!"

That was all Joe needed to say; one word uttered in disgust. His clamped jaw and narrowed eyes confirmed what she knew would come next.

"You know the policy here, and I don't bend the rules for anyone. I'll mail your last check." With that blunt announcement, he turned and headed to the grill.

Hanna stared at his back. Tears threaten to spill over the edge of her eyes. Even knowing Joe's zero tolerance policy for tardiness, the shock of his words, and what it meant for her immediate financial future, cut like a knife in her belly. Blinking back the tears, she fled the diner before anyone saw her embarrassment.

Judging by her furiously wagging tail, at least Bella was happy to see her back so soon. She licked Hanna's trembling fingers as she struggled to untie the leash from the shade tree.

"I've got myself in a terrible mess now, Bella. But don't worry, I promised Grandpa that I'd take good care of you until he's able to go home from the hospital. One thing I always do is keep a promise."

Bella's deep honey-colored fur under her hand felt silkier than the downy softness of a newly hatched chick. When she found the Golden Retriever's sensitive spot under her ear, the sixty-pound dog practically melted against Hanna's legs. Taking on Bella was the one bright light in her life at the moment. What do people say—when it rains, it pours? That described her situation. She wondered how many more hits she would have to endure. With her life an ugly tangled mess thanks to an abusive ex-boyfriend, she could now add no job to her troubles.

As Hanna walked away from the diner toward her small apartment with Bella trotting at her side, she considered the bright side—things could only improve from this low point. "You know, Bella, maybe I should look at this as a golden opportunity to get my life headed in a brand new direction."

Bella looked up at Hanna with her chocolate eyes and whined. Apparently, Grandpa had trained her well to tune into a person's mood and needs. At least, Hanna decided Bella's whine meant that she was adding encouragement to the conversation.

As cars whizzed by and trees swayed overhead,

Hanna continued to talk to her four-legged companion. It comforted her to know that someone, even if Bella was only a caring dog, was listening.

"Working for Joe was okay, but waiting on tables isn't what I want to do for the rest of my life anyway, and he didn't let me spend enough time baking pastries. That's what I love," she explained to Bella. "Maybe this is the push I need to come up with a plan for the rest of my life. No more excuses."

Bella woofed.

They continued at a comfortable pace—Hanna lost in her thoughts and Bella keeping close to her side.

Just as the noise of a revved up engine and screeching tires broke through Hanna's thoughts, her arm jerked so hard it felt like it was torn clean from its socket. She hit the pavement. Bits of gravel shredded her pants right into her skin, sending shocks of intense burning pain up her leg.

She lay still, gravel digging into one side of her face.

Bella licked her. She whined and pawed at Hanna's side.

Hanna groaned. "What happened?" she asked

her dog as she tried to gather herself up. Everything stung or ached or throbbed as she lay on the edge of the road. Her first thought was to move away from the traffic before someone ran her over.

Bella pulled on the leash hard enough to help Hanna half crawl, half slide onto the grass strip away from the whizzing cars. This spot would have to do until her head stopped spinning and she could stand and try to limp the rest of the way home.

Nothing made sense. Did a car hit her? She didn't think so, or she'd be in much worse shape. With the leash wrapped around her hand, and her shoulder screaming with pain, she decided that Bella must have yanked her out of harm's way. She tenderly felt the side of her head and winced.

"Is that what happened?" Hanna pushed herself to a sitting position with her good arm. "You pulled me out of harm's way?"

Bella curled up as close to Hanna as possible and set her big beautiful head in her lap.

"If only you could talk and tell me what happened." Hanna wrapped her arms around Bella's neck and cried into her fur at the reality of what could have been.

Now, she could add almost run over to her list of things going wrong in her life. Hanna slipped her phone from her pocket only to see several missed text messages. Her stomach clenched in a knot.

Seeing Greg's name pop up made everything worse. It had taken her too long to understand how obsessed he was with her. His recent rage chilled her to the bone. Dealing with him on top of everything else that hit her recently brought on more tears.

Bella lifted her head.

"Thank you for being here," Hanna said again. "I can count on you to be loyal even if it's hard to have trust in anyone else at the moment.

Her phone beeped with another text. She didn't open this one, either. She was so done with Greg, and it only made him angrier when she tried to explain why they couldn't be together. He said he'd made a mistake. Some mistake. When he grabbed her arm, leaving bruises in her tender flesh, he'd crossed a line. That action made it crystal clear that continuing any kind of relationship with Greg was not an option.

A car slowed, sending Hanna's heart racing.

Bella growled.

The passenger window lowered and an elderly woman gave her a friendly smile as she leaned across her front seat. "Are you okay, honey? That's really not the greatest place to sit and enjoy the weather."

Even though she hurt all over, Hanna chuckled at the ridiculous image others' must see of her on the side of the road hugging a dog. "You're right about that. Actually, someone almost hit me, and by the pain in my shoulder, I think my dog pulled me to safety."

"I live over there." The woman pointed to a house a few driveways back. "I couldn't believe what I was seeing when I got out of my car and looked over here. That golden blur dashed to one side with you flying behind. That's quite the dog you have. How about the two of you climb in and I'll take you to my house? I'll fix you some lemonade while you check your injuries and figure out who to call for help."

The kindness in the woman's voice made Hanna sniffle and hiccup. She wiped her nose. "Thanks. I'm Hanna, and this is Bella."

"Well, Hanna and Bella, I'm Geraldine, Gerri for short. Climb in and I'll get you off this road."

Hanna pushed herself upright with her good arm and opened the door. "Are you sure? I don't want to be any trouble."

"Trouble? You look like you've had more

trouble than you deserve, honey. I'm happy to lend a helping hand. Now, climb in before someone rear-ends me. These kids drive like the devil on this road."

Hanna let Bella into the back seat. Being careful not to jostle her shoulder, she managed to slide in next to Gerri.

"Slam that door good and hard or it might not catch properly. This car runs like a top even if it *is* older than the hills."

Gerri carefully checked the traffic then made a U-turn and pulled into a driveway not far from where she rescued Hanna.

"Is there someone you could call?" Gerri asked. "A pretty girl like you must have a boyfriend just dying to come to your rescue."

Hanna climbed out and Bella followed. Gerri's kindness was almost too much after all she'd been through this morning. Ignoring Gerri's question about a boyfriend, she said. "I'll just walk home. It's not far."

Gerri grabbed her arm. "I don't think so. You're in no shape to be walking anywhere. Haven't you learned your lesson about walking on this road? Come in and I'll make you some of my special lemonade while you figure out who to call for a ride."

Hanna said a silent thanks that Gerri didn't push her about a boyfriend. As kind as she seemed to be, that wasn't a subject she wanted to discuss. Especially with someone she'd only just met.

Gerri led the way into her tidy ranch house. Every surface had some sort of doily under an array of knickknacks. Porcelain dolls, carved cats, and delicate teacups filled floor to ceiling shelves. Not a safe space for a dog with a bushy, wagging tail.

"Oh no." Hanna managed to catch a carving of a wooden horse before it hit the floor when Bella's tail brushed over the coffee table.

Gerri laughed. "Don't worry. If a couple of these dust catchers break, I'll never miss them. I've got all my favorites tucked away out of harm's way."

Hanna giggled. Her emotions made the full swing from desperate to giddy now that she was safely off the road.

"Make yourself comfortable. I'll be back in a flash with lemonade for us and something for your friend." Gerri disappeared into what Hanna assumed was the doorway to her kitchen.

"This day is turning into something more interesting than I'd ever imagined," Hanna said to Bella. "Do you think it's safe to say that trouble is behind me and my life has turned the corner?"

Bella, with eyes like deep brown pools, searched Hanna's face. She wagged her tail as if letting Hanna know that whatever was to come, she'd be by her side. They were a team.

"You know," Gerri said when she returned with a tray filled to overflowing with enough lemonade and treats to feed the whole neighborhood, "something about that car that almost hit you is bothering me."

Hanna hadn't given the car a second thought as she lay on the side of the road, bruised and scared. "What do you mean?"

"Well," Gerri poured lemonade into two dainty cups, "I'd swear it swerved right toward you. If Bella hadn't pulled you out of harm's way, I don't think you'd be sitting here with me enjoying this lemonade."

Want to keep reading? Head to
www.SweetPromisePress.com/GoldCoast to
grab your copy now!

What's our Sweet Promise? It's to deliver the heartwarming, entertaining, clean, and wholesome reads you love with every single book.

From contemporary to historical romances to suspense and even cozy mysteries, all of our books are guaranteed to put a song in your heart and a smile on your face. That's our promise to you, and we can't wait to deliver upon it...

We release one new book per week, which means the flow of sweet, relatable reads coming your way never ends. Make sure to save some space on your eReader!

Check out our books in Kindle Unlimited at
sweetpromisepress.com/Unlimited

More from Sweet Promise

Pre-order upcoming series bundles to save at
sweetpromisepress.com/Shop

Join our reader discussion group, meet our authors,
and make new friends at
sweetpromisepress.com/Group

Sign up for our weekly newsletter at
sweetpromisepress.com/Subscribe

And don't forget to like us on Facebook at
sweetpromisepress.com/FB

Six special Golden Retrievers help their humans solve mysteries, save lives, and even find love...

Saving Sarah by Melissa Storm

Sarah Campbell loves living vicariously through the residents at the Redwood Cove Rest Home. But when a surly patient insists she can't die before "setting things right," Sarah finds she may end up taking on far more than she ever bargained for... especially since all signs point to murder. Have she and her therapy dog Lucky stumbled upon the key to solving the most famous cold case in Gold Coast history?

Despite creating the world's most popular social network, Finch Jameson lives a life of ashamed solitude. The last thing he wants is to draw attention to himself, but that's exactly what happens when a distant relative delivers an earth-shattering confession in her dying days. Soon he finds himself more intrigued by the shy and beautiful nurse who's committed to helping him solve his great-aunt Eleanor's mystery than in the mystery itself. But will she ever let her guard down long enough to let him in?

Can Finch and Sarah work together to solve Eleanor's big mystery before time runs out? And might redeeming Eleanor's legacy somehow save them both in the process?

Get your copy at
SweetPromisePress.com/GoldCoast

RESCUING RILEY BY S.B. ALEXANDER

Riley Lewis may plan weddings for a living, but it doesn't mean she believes in love. However, love may be just what she gets when she lays eyes on the disabled veteran running the bed and breakfast that will serve as her home during a much-needed visit with her best friend.

Joshua Bandon wanted one thing when he was discharged from the military—peace and quiet. But when his service dog, Charlie, falls hard for a beautiful woman staying at their inn, he just may end up following suit.

When Riley's best friend disappears without warning, Josh and Charlie may be the only ones who can help... Especially when Riley goes missing too.

***Get your copy at
SweetPromisePress.com/GoldCoast***

Guarding Grace by Ann Omasta

Grace Wilson loves the wonderful life she has created with her daughter in picturesque Redwood Cove, California—even if she is a bit lonely. To add to their family, mom and daughter adopt a sweet

More from this Series

"Golden Wetweevuh" puppy. And they're not the only ones who think Star is, well, a star. A television show casts the pup for a role, but it's the co-host that has Grace's heart doing tricks.

Dash Diamond is a local celebrity with a megawatt smile. He is less than thrilled when his show's producers inform him that a puppy has been cast in a new role. But his new co-star comes with an owner who makes Dash see stars when he looks at her.

When Star is puppy-napped and held for ransom, all attention goes to her rescue. Grace and Dash can't act on their undeniable romantic spark of attraction while the pup is possibly in danger. Star is the missing piece. Will they find her in time to complete their puzzle?

Get your copy at
SweetPromisePress.com/GoldCoast

Protecting Peyton by Becky Muth

Peyton McIntyre's brother is missing. Local police claim they're looking into it, but hope dwindles as

More from this Series

the days continue to pass without any answers. Worse still, her only chance of finding him may depend on a rookie officer who sends her temper flaring and her heart quivering.

Kurt Collins is a fourth-generation police officer, but so far he hasn't been able to live up to his family's long legacy of service. When the infuriating and beautiful Peyton asks for his help, he wonders if she might hold the key to the recognition he craves. Last time they met, her dog, Gilda, saved his life. This time she just might be able save his reputation.

As they begin their search it appears that Peyton's brother may not want to be found. Unfortunately, failing to complete this assignment could risk both Kurt's career and any chance he has at winning Peyton's heart. Is a happy ending even possible, or will Peyton and Kurt both lose everything before they're through?

Get your copy at
SweetPromisePress.com/GoldCoast

FINDING FELICITY BY P. CREEDEN

More from this Series

Despite a difficult childhood, Felicity Stilton never gave up on her dreams. Now, as an adult, she and her Golden Retriever, JJ, help special needs children pave the way for their own futures. Everything is perfect, until she gets the one call she never expected to receive.

Officer Darren Willis hates that it falls to him to tell the beautiful and inspiring Felicity her birth mother has taken her own life. Although the case appears to be open-and-shut, the grieving daughter insists something foul is afoot. Will he be brave enough to follow dark clues into the past along side the one woman with whom he just might want to make a future?

Only Darren believes Felicity's suspicions and is willing to help investigate what really happened to her long-lost mother. When the signs begin to point to murder, Darren worries Felicity might be next… But should he abandon the case to protect her even if it means losing the woman he loves forever?

Get your copy at
SweetPromisePress.com/GoldCoast

More from this Series

HELPING HANNA BY EMMIE LYN

For Hanna Moss, love has always come with danger. From the incessant stalking by an ex to nearly losing her life in a hit and run accident, she vows to remain alone--and safe. So when her golden retriever, Bella, welcomes a handsome private investigator into their lives Hanna is surprised to find herself willing to open up despite the tremendous risks that have always come with letting others in.

Blake Bowman returns to Redwood Cove with a shattered heart. All he wants is to enjoy a much-needed quiet vacation far from his ex-girlfriend. At least, that was the plan until he meets Hanna—beautiful and with an injury that is more than skin deep. He'll need to stay focused, though, because it looks like what happened to her was no accident.

Blake desperately wants to help Hanna in every way possible, even if that means putting love on hold. Hanna is terrified of the feelings she's rapidly developing for Blake and refuses to repeat her past mistakes... Is Hanna safer on her own, or will trusting Blake finally allow her to heal?

Find out if Bella can help these two humans understand that trust is a two-way street, that the heart can be repaired, and that love can bloom again. This sweet romance is sure to shine the light of love into your life... Order your copy and start reading today!

Get your copy at
SweetPromisePress.com/GoldCoast

About the Author

P. Creeden is the sweet romance and mystery pen name for USA Today Bestselling Author Pauline Creeden. She loves a good mystery and grew up watching Colombo, Perry Mason, and Murder, She Wrote. Books have always been a focal point of her life, from Nancy Drew and Sir Arthur Conan Doyle to thrillers like John Sanford.

Animals are the supporting characters of many of her stories, because they occupy her daily life on the farm, too. From dogs, cats, and goldfish to horses, chickens, and geckos -- she believes life around pets is so much better, even if they are fictional. P. Creeden married her college sweetheart, who she also met at a horse farm. Together they raise a menagerie of animals and their one son, an avid reader, himself.

If you enjoyed this story, look forward to more books by P. Creeden.

In 2018, she plans to release more than twelve new books!

Hear about her newest release, FREE books when they come available, and giveaways hosted by the author—subscribe to her newsletter: https://www.subscribepage.com/pcreedenbooks

---

If you enjoyed this book and want to help the author, consider leaving a review at your favorite book seller – or tell someone about it on social media. Authors live by word of mouth!

CPSIA information can be obtained
at www.ICGtesting.com
Printed in the USA
LVHW081434131118
596975LV00015B/833/P